# MENSONGE

*Also by Malcolm Bradbury*

FICTION
Eating People is Wrong
Stepping Westward
The History Man
Who Do You Think You Are?
The After Dinner Game (television plays)
Rates of Exchange
Cuts: A Very Short Novel

CRITICISM
Evelyn Waugh
What is a Novel?
The Social Context of Modern English Literature
Possibilities
Saul Bellow
The Modern American Novel
No, Not Bloomsbury

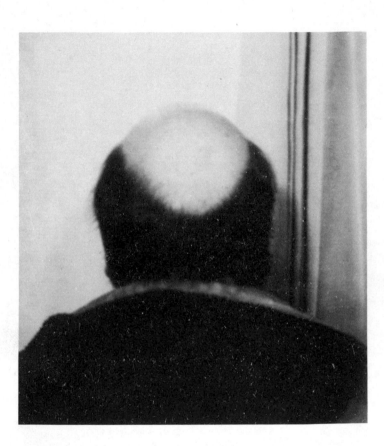

The only known extant photograph of Mensonge. He is believed to be contemplating a distant prospect of the Café Flore.
*(Photographer, T.G. Rosenthal?)*

*My Strange Quest for*

# MENSONGE

*Structuralism's
Hidden Hero*

Malcolm Bradbury

with a Foreword/Afterword
by Michel Tardieu
*(Professor of Structuralist Narratology,
University of Paris)*

translated by David Lodge

ANDRE DEUTSCH

First published in 1987 by André Deutsch Ltd
105-106 Great Russell Street, London WC1B 3LJ

ISBN 0 233 98020 2

Phototypeset by Falcon Graphic Art Ltd
Wallington, Surrey
Printed in Great Britain by
Ebenezer Baylis & Son Ltd, Worcester

'What difference does it make who is speaking?'
Michel Foucault, 'What Is an Author?'

# 1

There can be no doubt that any bright student or intellectually active person of the 1980s who is at all alert to the major developments in the humanities, philosophy and the social sciences, or is just getting more and more worried why so many way-out mint-flavoured green vegetables are showing up in a salad these days, is going sooner or later, and far better sooner than later, to have to come to terms with a pair of thought-movements that are making all the contemporary running. These twin thought-movements are, as most people now know, called Structuralism and Deconstruction. These movements have spoken to what even the *Guardian* newspaper has identified as our 'postmodern condition' – a state of affairs where, in the wake of the Holocaust and in an era of terrible nuclear anxiety, we not only lose all hope in technological, social and human progress but start wearing green Liberty scarves as well. They are, like most good thought-movements, French in origin, and many of the finest Gallic minds have added a part to their making, their refinement, their complication, and their texture. They belong in the great tradition of Plato and Aristotle, Spinoza and Leibnitz, Berkeley and Locke, Kant and Hegel, Kierkegaard and Heidegger, though they can truly be said to have a Gallic flavour or *frisson* all their own. Like any truly serious philosophical movement, they are quite hard to find out about, still harder to understand, and yet harder still to become a full master, or mistress, of. This should not surprise us. Thinking, these days, is a complex matter, the history is hard, the new technology difficult, the stakes being raised all the time. Nor does what is happening within the strict church of philosophy always reach the outside world.

Information-gathering on what is happening is patchy and imperfect, as is often the way with a quickly changing field, and much of what we hear murmured by those who claim to be on the inside is far from accurate. Philosophy these days requires virtuoso qualities, and the star performers are not themselves always cooperative, a classic problem with very deep thinkers. The labels we hear are not necessarily those accepted by the masters themselves. Michel Foucault, the great radical historian, insisted until quite recently, when he died, that he was not a Structuralist, but something quite different along the same lines. Likewise to the question, 'Just where and how does the Deconstructionist philosopher Jacques Derrida stand?', there is and can be no simple or clear-cut answer.

Yet a self-evidently major movement in contemporary thought is bound to attract enormous public attention. And people everywhere, many of whom would regard themselves as at best amateurs in philosophy, and some of whom have not thought for years, have grown alert to the importance of the new tendencies, naturally not wanting to miss out on something a lot of other people are talking about and are likely to go on talking about for generations to come. In fact, and to be honest, there is no doubt that Structuralism-Deconstruction has become, to say the least, *chic*, and the title 'designer philosophy' that some people have given it is, though unfair, not totally off the target. *People* magazine was showing only the other week not only how many leading Structuralists like to dine at Sardi's these days, often on very experimental diets, but how they probably started the entire Perrier revolution, while Hollywood columnists have spotted several Deconstructionists playing royal tennis with Joan Collins. Spielberg is known to be interested, and there is talk of a major film set among Deconstructionists, exploring their complex thought-practices, laidback life-styles and unusual sexual mores and what happens to them when they quit Paris and hit the trail for Texas; Robert Redford is said to be interested in the Derrida role if it can be played as an American. Structuralist tie-ins are showing up in the yuppie boutiques, I notice, and tee-shirts saying 'Foucault' and mugs saying 'This is not (or is it?) a mug' are there in all the teenage bed-and-romp rooms from Minsk to California. Apart from high-speed bicycling and supply-side economics, the new French philosophy is probably the most talked-over scene of the last three years. Its impact spreads everywhere, even into the most unexpected places. It is thanks to one of its major offshoots, semiology, or the science of signs, that it is no longer possible to enter a public lavatory and be at all sure one's companions will be of the same sex. It is *merci* to another of its offshoots, *nouvelle cuisine*, or *cuisine minceur*, that we have all learned to regard restaurant food as an art-object, or plated Mondrian. Novels have been made obscure in its name, and those strange passages on film or television where the camera moves in to someone's head of hair and we realize we have just been flashbacked twenty years are a sign or semiotic of the pervasive influence of Structuralism. There is no doubt that we do live in a Structuralist- or Deconstructionist-shaped universe.

On the other hand, as Bob Geldof was pointing out just the other day, what Structuralism and Deconstruction actually mean *epistemologically* could do with much further clarification. This book provides us all with the opportunity for that wider understanding. We must remember, of course, that, especially given the way they are designing jeans these days, great thought does not fit easily into pockets. Nor is it easy to describe by the usual means, language, the essential message of the whole tendency, which is that we live in a Crisis of Nomination – which is to say that not only can we no longer effectively name things but we cannot even be sure they were there in the first place. What we have to remember is that, in the sphere of philosophy, as of everything else, obscurity is there for a purpose, and not to confuse us. As Immanuel Kant observed, it is the nature of man as thinking animal that he be constantly up the creek of being and knowing without any certainty of the existence of even the simplest paddle.

The effort is nonetheless worthwhile, for the simple reason that this radical new spirit in intellectual life touches on every aspect of existence, social and cultural, literary and artistic, linguistic and anthropological. Indeed it has been so successful

3

that it is capitalizing its resources and spreading out into totally new areas, including cheap home-loans and cut-price airlines. We all have colleagues in academic life – at least, most of us do not, but I do – who have tried to ignore the entire issue, keeping their heads in the sand and their noses high in the air. Whether through ignorance, obscurantism, or simply not having been, like some of us, in the right place at the right time, they have chosen to believe that the whole issue will in due course disappear, and we will soon be back in the safety of empirical common sense again. I have to tell these people (I name no names, but I think they know just exactly who they are, which indeed proves at once they are not Structuralists) that they will have to think again, if they are at all capable of it. We have burned our boats, cut ourselves adrift, dispensed with the old reality, and are now on a voyage of discovery sailing to the *terra nova* of the changed dispensation. As François Mitterrand was heard to say the other day, teasing at a shrimp *vol-au-vent* at some Quai d'Orsay reception to do with either the building or the cancellation of the Channel Tunnel: 'Aujourd'hui, mes amis, et aussi les anglais, nous sommes tous de nécessité structuralistes.'

And we may take it Mitterrand's statement was true, or as true as true is in a time when, thanks to Deconstruction, truth is very much an open question. For it is quite certain that these two separate yet related tendencies – later in this book I will explain just how we go about the difficult and delicate task of separating yet relating them – are *our* philosophy, *our* condition, *our* crisis and *our* promise, and we cannot say nay to them. Whether we realize it or not, they dominate the flavour of life and thinking in the last quarter of the twentieth century just as Existentialism did in the third quarter. They are, in the realm of cognition, what Texas is to California in the realm of growth potential and property values, but with the added advantage of not being directly oil-related. Where Existentialism was intense and heavy, strong on plight and anguish, Structuralism-Deconstruction, in keeping with the times, is clean absurdism or cool philosophy; it is laid back, requires no weighty black gear, and goes very well with Perrier water and skiing.

It is also the philosophy that goes along with everything else we know so well now – our chiliasm, our apocalypticism, our post-humanist scepticism, our postmodernism, our metaphysical exhaustion, our taste for falafel. After all, we find ourselves, in these strange times, the children not just of the end of a bitter and war-torn century, in which the great hopes raised by the new science have turned sour upon us, leaving behind little but the invention of the pill and a few buildings by Richard Rogers, but of an entire millennium, almost a thousand years long, of Christian and post-Christian Western history. We know that the great burst of human thought and skill that produced the Dark Ages and the Renaissance, the Enlightenment and Abstract Expressionism, that was capable of discovering capitalist individualism, evolution, the unconscious, relativity, nuclear fission, space travel and the fifteen-speed bicycle, is coming to the end of its term. Today Christian charity, capitalist individualism, and humanistic utopianism are all reaching the close of their useful lives, leaving a very large hole in thinking that could be extremely dangerous if neglected. Fortunately into this hole the philosophies of Structuralism and Deconstruction have now stepped.

So here, then, are the movements which are to us what Cartesianism was to the seventeenth century, and consciousness-raising and aerobic breathing to the 1970s. They declare the bankruptcy of our entire philosophical condition. They reveal our fundamental loss of coherence and the disappearance amongst us of any sense of truth or reality. They display our nullity, and our plenitude. They also give us a very exciting new way of reading Wordsworth's *The Prelude*. We should not under-estimate, as in an off-moment we could so easily do, the magnitude of the message this philosophical revolution – and it is nothing less – is bringing us. It is telling us that we are indeed coming to a terminus of thought, reaching *the end of signification*. It is showing us that just as we can no longer get a competently produced free-range egg or an honest dollar, so we cannot obtain *a proper sign*. It is proving beyond doubt that we find ourselves in *the age of the floating signifier*, when word no longer attaches properly to thing, and no highbonding glues can help us. It discloses to us a world of parody and pastiche, query and quotation; and having shown us all this, it teaches us how to enjoy it.

The massive consequences of this message cannot be overlooked. What this means is that for two thousand years at least people have been able to conduct business, and even pleasure, in the knowledge that they knew who they were, and what the reality out there was, that they meant what they said and knew what they saw, even if they acknowledged the old epistemological problem on very foggy days. Over that two thousand years, an entire lineage of philosophy, starting in the Eastern Mediterranean, spread westward and northward through then primeval forests by very bad routes, some of them still in use today, to bring home to people the notions of monotheism and conscience, deism and transcendentalism, the bases of Western culture. The thought enlarged to incorporate evolutionism, materialism, scientism, psychologism, and then modern relativism, existentialism and Kierkegaardian fear-and-trembling. Yet it all had a common basis founded on the mind–body dichotomy, sometimes called the Cartesian *cogito*, though at other times not. Through it we learned, in a series of prodigious feats, how to dominate nature, build culture, master the organization and structure of the universe, invent the collar stud and discover how to use the cellular telephone. We also learned how to write string quartets and make a fairly good *soufflé*, so perhaps it has not all been wasted.

But this tradition depended on a stable concept of the self, and a reasonably firm notion of a reality *out there*, dense enough for us to be able at least to drive a nail into it, and hang up a picture when required. It is nothing less than this entire tradition that Structuralism and Deconstruction are helping to bring to an end, opening up new but confusing opportunities. In this it has been the culmination of a process. Karl Marx demystified capitalist ideology, and showed how history worked, if we followed the instructions properly. Sigmund Freud undermined the rational ego, and showed us how the Unconscious functioned, which was in ways that surprised some people but quite excited others. Albert Einstein undermined traditional science, showing that the world was a non-Euclidian four-dimensional space-time continuum, probably only held together by its railways. Now Structuralism and Deconstruction have come along to complete the process, demythologizing, demystifying and *deconstructing* our entire basis of thought, and suggesting other ways to use it. They have required us to redefine all our values and transform all our epistemologies, or at the very least to take a two-week holiday in the sun with someone we love very much and work out all future priorities very carefully. They have dismantled our preconceived framework of consciousness and perception, removed all our ideas of the transcendent and the everlasting, and dismantled the concept of the 'subject', or, as it used to be known, in the old days, the person, so making table-setting for a dinner party very difficult indeed. They have done this by challenging our sense of essence and reality at its very root, *in language*, proving to us that it is not working – or certainly not in the way it was meant to when people in caves started grunting at each other and thought this would establish quite clearly just who would go out and do the shopping.

In brief, Structuralism and Deconstruction are and remain important because they have quite simply disestablished *the entire basis of human discourse*. This cannot be overlooked; for example, it has left those of us who, like myself, have just gone out and invested large sums in expensive word-processing equipment with a good deal of egg on our faces. The consequences reach everywhere. They affect the basis of our art and our culture, explaining just why it is that books make less sense than before and paintings are coming out of the canvas and have already started giftwrapping California. It has changed all our basic practices, like those of law and medicine, showing that doctors do not really know what we are saying and that we should sue them, just so long as we can find a lawyer who is in any better shape. They affect our attitudes to sex and gender at the root, showing that sexual identity is really role-typing, and the only real difference between people is not whether they are men or women but whether they are little or big. Now they are working on the right kind of fibre we need in our diet. The impact of this will in due course be massive, meaning nothing less than that it will be necessary to *re-write everything*. Happily this will take time, and just for the moment the instructions on a jar of instant coffee still remain more or less usable, though we cannot count on it, any more than we can or should on anything else in this increasingly difficult world.

# 2

Not for a long time in our human history – perhaps not since the Greeks first looked up from their ouzo and started to speculate about the meaning of the universe around them – has so remarkable a revolution in human thought occurred as the one I have been describing; and many people are asking just why it should happen now, and to us, though quite a few I meet are for some reason not. But to understand these matters clearly, it is necessary to ask ourselves just *how* this great revolution occurred, just *who* is responsible for it, and exactly *what* should we do to them if we ever succeed in tracing them? Inevitably the answers to these questions are profound and complex, and they certainly take us back to the beginnings of Indo-European civilization and probably also to the Greek city-states; however travel that way is expensive and would require the assistance of research grants of a scale I have come nowhere near to getting. Hence, if we content ourselves with a rather briefer answer, we will do best to take ourselves back to the radical, modernizing years of the early part of this century, and the terrible trench warfare of the First World War – or rather to the nearby city of Geneva at the same time, where, to be frank, it is a good deal safer.

For the Switzerland of World War I was the great haven of our modern intellectual revolution. In frosty Zürich, up the road, James Joyce was writing *Ulysses*, Tristan Tzara inventing Dada, and Lenin planning the Russian Revolution, all watched by the then very young Tom Stoppard. But in Geneva the book that stopped the trams and caused an intellectual furore was a work

8

of linguistics, Ferdinand de Saussure's *Cours de linguistique générale*, which he published in 1916, for some reason post-humously, since the author himself had died three years before without writing it. The book was the record of a course of lectures Saussure had given to his impressed and often baffled students at the University of Geneva between 1907 and 1911, and which were to upturn all ideas of the nature of language. Saussure argued that every sign had two parts, a *langue* and a *parole*, which could be separated, so allowing us to understand how language works or, in practice, does not. In the event, the great proof of Saussure's argument came with the publication of his book. Saussure himself having died before he wrote it down, its text was retrieved from the various notes and doodles of his students – some of them a little inconsistent, probably due to the people horsing around on the back row. Anyone who has actually seen a student taking notes in a lecture will know how hard it is to connect what is actually said with what is being written down, and none of us can be sure that the *Cours* actually comes near to recording what Saussure meant – indeed we cannot know whether he would actually have acknowledged a single *langue* or *parole* of it, or be able to explain where the drawing of the rabbit actually fits. In fact we may regard the book Saussure 'wrote' – which of course he actually did not – as the strongest piece of evidence we have of the argument the book itself makes, about the separation of the signifier from the signified.

For what Saussure proved – or so his students seemed to think – was that words were arbitrary, and hence that in effect everything had been given the wrong name, so that horses were really fish and fish onions. All signs were actually random, though they had the capacity to make sense, except possibly at Heathrow Airport. A gap exists between the words we speak, and what language, behaving like language, actually gets up to when we are not keeping a proper eye on it. Hence there is *langue*, which is more or less what allows us to talk, and there is also *parole*, which explains why nobody bothers to listen. To illustrate all this, Saussure used as his famous example the 8.25 Geneva-to-Paris Express, which, as he pointed out, retained the same name and was considered the same train every day, even though its coaches, combination, crew and passengers were different every morning, most of the coaches did not go to Paris, and it usually left at 10.30. So famous did this example become after Saussure's book came out in 1916 that people went down every day to the station to check it, only to discover that the train had been cancelled because of the war. And this of course only further proved, or possibly disproved, Saussure's point – that there was indeed a gap between *langue* and *parole*, and possibly a bigger one than even he had noticed.

Indeed gaps were very important in the new Saussurian linguistics, as they have been ever since. For Saussure established that the gap between *langue* and *parole* was actually based on an even larger gap, between what he called the *signifier*, or *signifiant*, and the *signified*, or *signifié*. It is very important to understand the difference between these two terms, or I fear we shall never be able to have a proper Structuralist conversation. The signifier can be briefly explained as the sound we make when we seek to make reference to a signified, while a signified is the thing we think of when we think we hear a signifier – as long as it is spoken loudly enough and preferably not in Old Norse. Since the relation between these two can be regarded as totally arbitrary, except possibly in Japanese, this made speaking and writing into extremely improbable pastimes. He was equally helpful in the formulation of some other useful gaps that no one had thought of before, like that between the *diachronic* and the *synchronic*, which we would do well not to forget. (Essentially the difference is that diachronic change occurs in an evolutionary order, while synchronic change happens all at the same time for no good reason.) By adding some more terms, like *syntagmatic* and *paradigmatic*, Saussure made a great deal possible, including the British Council. Indeed with the invention of what Saussure called *Homo significans*, or Man the Sign-Maker, the whole course of modern history was changed. Italian foreign-language students started filling the streets and pubs of Cambridge, new ways of teaching language became possible, and everyone began talking wafl about TEFL. And here began the history of Structuralism and Deconstruction – a history that has been fairly described as the development from Saussure to not saussure at all.

10

In the postwar years it was soon apparent that the new linguistic science was having an international impact on every form of thought. A decisive step was the formation of the famous Prague School, which met in that city for the First International Congress of Slavic Philologists in 1929, consistently found themselves directed to the wrong rooms, and were hence in a position to confirm definitely that there was a clear gap between the signifier and the signified – though not quite so large a gap as hypothesized by those who for some reason supposed the congress was actually being held in Vienna, met in a city square and formed the even more daring Vienna Circle, which could not find itself at all thereafter. This was not surprising, for war clouds were gathering again. The great linguistic revolution, which sent its radiating influence throughout the Western world, found its development interrupted by a Second World War, which broke up most of the circles, bombed the squares in which they met, interrupted yet again the Geneva–Paris Express, and scattered the linguists in all directions. The Prague School now found itself largely in Britain while the Vienna Circle was largely in the United States. Thus the linguistic method spread everywhere, and once the war was over grammatological revolution resumed. And it is now that begins the high point of our story, at a new time, the late 1950s and 1960s, and in a new city, the world's great intellectual hothouse, Paris itself. It is to that city we must look for the next crucial stage of the matter – or rather not simply to Paris, but one particular, famous *milieu* within it, none other than the famous *rive gauche*, or Left Bank.

So it is here – in the heart of the famous fifth *arrondissement*, the historical part of Paris which contains not only the Sorbonne, the Bibliothèque Nationale, the Luxembourg Gardens, but most of the French riot police and innumerable establishments devoted to that odd culinary delicacy the French hamburger – that we must go to see the final separation of the signifier from the signified: the spectacular and final fracture out of which the Structuralist and Deconstructionist movement was born. It was a birth that took some forty years, and this *quartier*, Montparnasse, or the Latin Quarter, was a natural lying-in place for the momentous parturition. For here was one of the great cradles of human thought and radical vision. On the *terrasses* of the great cafés, the Rotonde, the Profonde, the Lipp and the Deux Magots, writers and painters, thinkers and *poules* had sat for countless generations, writing, painting, thinking and clucking, staring and shouting abuse at the passing throng, and waiting for the *garçon* to turn up finally with their drink. Here Picasso resolved to paint the portrait of Gertrude Stein, so inventing Cubism. Here Tzara's Dada met with Breton's Nada, causing a confusion which has still not quite settled. Here, over a bock, Hemingway wrote his one true sentence, Pound cut *The Waste Land* down to size, and Joyce met Beckett and generously asked him to translate *Finnegans Wake* into French, an act of friendship most of us have been fortunate to have been spared. Here philosophy flourished and the great French tradition of *clarté* reached its high refinement, though more in the mornings than the afternoons. Deep in the heart of this romantic and bohemian *quartier* there lies the Rue des Ecoles, that narrow intellectual street close to the old Sorbonne where Voltaire and Diderot, Pound and Eliot, Stein and Hemingway, Joyce and Beckett, all walked, rubbing their shoulders together and blocking the traffic for hours. And it was here, in the spirit of the radical, revolutionary 1960s, when everything was, as they like to say in Paris, up for the grabs, that the great change came.

For now was born, from the high-minded dialectics and disputations of the new *philosophes* of a truly turbulent time, that way of thinking – as hermeneutic as it was hermetic, as post-Husserlian as it was neo-Hegelian – which, as the leading thinker Michel Foucault was in due course to point out, disestablished all the existing paradigms of knowledge and changed once and for all the entire order of things. At first not everyone was ready to agree with Foucault. Indeed there were many people only too glad to mock him, and they could often be heard shouting his name after him in the street in a quite dismissive way. Of course he was right, and they were wrong, for we know this is not a story of losers. What started as a local argument among the Parisian exegetes soon began to spread its Structuralist tentacles through every department of human thought, from linguistics to anthropology, from philosophy to psycho-analysis, historiography to literary studies, until at last, as these things do at last, it finally reached the department of driver education. It was done. Clearly there was a new ideology, a latter-day *summa*, or, as Foucault put it far more clearly, a new *episteme*.

The revolution kept on revolving, and by the mid-1960s it had clearly captured the entire Gallic intellectual scene, as Yale University is sometimes called. By the decade's end the news was everywhere, even reaching to Great Britain, a nation not notable for its acceptance of new philosophies, unless they say something very cogent about soccer. After Yale came Princeton, Johns Hopkins and Cornell, and there were murmurings at Harvard. In Britain Structuralist cells of a vestigial kind were reported in segments of East Anglia, and entire districts of Islington. Even at Oxford, the language philosophers were forced to pause for a moment in their long-time consideration of whether the other side of the moon was, is, or ever will be made of green cheese to acknowledge the issue, albeit briefly. More dramatically, at Cambridge the entire English faculty suddenly erupted in uproar and internecine strife over this extraordinary new matter. The issue, fanned by the popular press and an opportunist Labour party, even came to threaten the government, and risk the stability of the pound sterling, until, happily, serious conflict broke out in the Falkland Islands and it was possible to divert public attention away from the crisis and back towards football. Even so, a good deal of blood had been spilled, most of it, fortunately, only metaphorical.

So, by the middle of the 1970s, the Structuralist and thereafter the Deconstructionist affair was, as we have shown, creating that worldwide upheaval in thinking that has made it inescapable for anyone who cares to have a thought about anything. The burning flames of intellectual change had everywhere been fanned. Western intellectuals grew used to receiving calls, usually very late at night, and always collect, from their philosophical counterparts in Moscow or Tashkent, Beijing or Saigon, as even Marxist intellectuals began to see the transforming force of this new post-ideology. The key principles of Structuralism – that thought and culture are not transcendental

13

entities but can only be understood as structures of power and domination, so requiring that philosophy dispose of its old interests to some innocent buyer and at once become a science of signs, and that you cannot trust the trains – were being accepted everywhere, except possibly in Iran and certain parts of Tennessee. Intellectuals throughout the globe thus now had to sit down and discriminate their *langues* from their *paroles*, their signifiers from their signifieds, their diachronics from their synchronics, their Erse from their Igbo, their generative grammar from their transformational grammar, and some of them are known to have changed their lectures almost entirely.

What Saussure had started one day in his study in Geneva was now a worldwide force. Everywhere it was clear that the old ways of thinking, based on the mind–body dichotomy and the stable foundation of language, would no longer do. The day of the Cartesian *cogito* was over, or certainly getting toward its dusk. It was plain that far from thought being written in language language was writing thought, and not doing it well. No longer did Descartes's famous dictum, 'I think, therefore I am,' serve; he was wrong in both respects. As one of the leading new gurus, the psycho-analytic Structuralist Jacques Lacan, was to explain: 'I think where I am not, therefore I am where I do not think.' Evidently, if thinking of any sort were to survive, it would have to be begun all over again, performed by quite different means, and normally when one happened to be somewhere else at the time. All thought practices and all ways of saying were in question; the world was in a new crisis of knowing, an epistemological quandary. This could well have been confusing, but like most trouble it was quickly accepted as the new order of things. As with so many revolutions, what one week seemed a fundamental challenge to everything became the stuff of commonplace pedagogy the next.

By the beginning of the 1980s students everywhere, from Harvard to Heidelberg, Cambridge to Canton, Oxford to Oslo, Vienna to Vincennes, Yale to Jyvaskyla, were going to their classes thinking the new thoughts and carrying with them the new texts, or rather anti-texts, the texts that said that all the texts except these particular texts were dead. Courses that had once

14

spent the entire semester studying the mode of irony in Jane Austen's *Emma* soon took up with extraordinary new practices, exploring the fine detail of such books as Foucault's monumental, multi-volumed *The History of Sexuality*, or its less well-known sequel *The History of Sleep*, Claude Lévi-Strauss's *The History of Table Manners*, or Roland Barthes's *The Pleasure of the Text*. More advanced classes studied Jacques Derrida's *Glas* (translated into English as *Glas*) or Jacques Lacan's *Ecrits* (translated into English as, of course, *Ecrits*). A great new pantheon of philosophical folk-heroes and folk-heroines began to appear, the movers and shakers of the new thought. There were many other new names – Althusser and Kristeva, Baudrillard and Lyotard, Harold Bloom and Thomas Kuhn, Jacques Lacan and Paul de Man – though, as we shall see, not all the most important of the radical new figures hit the consciousness of the ever-growing number of new fans of philosophy.

Thus the great revolution was complete. The acolytes and latter-day interpreters appeared, and the handbooks and breviaries of explication and explanation multiplied, totally driving the sex-manuals of the 1970s off the shelves. Tome after tome appeared on Structuralism and Deconstruction, and one has now to struggle past them in any good bookstore anywhere in the world in order to find some actual books. Nearly all, but not all, of the major texts were translated out of their French-resembling originals into a something that has often been compared with or described as English. Everywhere people engaged in the study of signs, often starting by first trying to find out how to reach the library. Methods of teaching changed, linguistics became a growth subject, and there was an enormous transformation in grammar.

Now that we no longer knew quite what things meant any more, a new method in the study of literature called creative misreading, or maps of misprision, began, as it were, to bloom. It abolished authors, and replaced them by readers, who turned out to need a lot of critics to help them misunderstand in the proper way. The flag under which all now marched was Pierre Macheray's 'Let us say, provisionally, that the critic, employing a new language, brings out a *difference* in the work by demonstrating that it is *other than it is*,' or Derrida's 'Reading is freed from the horizon of the meaning or truth of being, liberated from the values of the product's production or the present's presence,' two useful statements that permit us all a great deal, if not everything. But no longer was it necessary to confine critical reading to literature, and new studies in entire new areas from the cereal packet to the Peanuts cartoon now began to develop, mostly in the London polytechnics. The wind of change was blowing everywhere, and the day of the modern reader who did not need a book at all was born.

This required a whole new look at the entire tradition of thought and writing, and the great unmasking of the errors of the past by the misreadings of the present proceeded apace. Not only did the new theory prove that the cupboard of Western thought was now bare; it showed it had always been *completely empty in the first place*. Now was the time to demystify and denude, revealing to the world that not only the emperor but every single one of his subjects was either not wearing clothes at all, or did so only because they had been role and gender-typed. Stripping and tearing, the new philosophy grew decidedly erotic, in ways that Kant would probably not even have begun to understand, or not until after a quite extensive explanation, ideally in German. Nor was the new revolution purely a campus matter. The new desire represented by Deconstruction began spreading everywhere, from study to living room, kitchen and bedroom. It was not long before everyone was really into Structuralist furniture, called *bricolage*, or Do-It-Yourself. There was a great revolution of Structuralist cooking, *nouvelle cuisine* or *la révolution mange-tout*, where Structuralist principles would be presented in a pleasant music-filled ambiance and with the choice of Thousand Island or Rocquefort dressing. There was Structuralist sex, based on the disappearance of the subject, so it was no longer clear who is the who who is doing what with what to whom's whom, and Structuralist *haute couture*, where dresses are silk and still have the hangers in them, but upside down. Whoever we were, or were not, one thing was certain: Structuralism and Deconstruction were now nothing less than *state of the art*, the real bottom line of thinking wherever thinking was being done in the truly modern world of today.

# 3

And there then we have it, the history and significance of the Structuralist and Deconstructionist revolution, for certainly it is nothing less. Yet like most revolutions it has been a matter of strange passages, lost leaders and striking ironies. Once again it has established French thinking as quite the best kind of thinking there is, renewing the credit and the credibility of thirty-odd years ago, when one could not enter the most provincial coffee bar without hearing talk of Sartre and Camus. Like the finest French vintages – with which, it must be admitted, the leading participants are from time to time confused – the great names and the finest labels of the movement are spoken of everywhere, though as with the wines not all those who know the labels seem entirely aware of the contents of the bottles. Like the best French *couture*, the tags speak not only of quality but the very highest *chic*, and are safe guarantees that one is getting not thought off the peg but the best possible design in the field of ratiocination. Today it would be foolish, or decidedly unsmart, to attend any congress or cocktail party in the great cities of the world, and not be able to parry a Lacan with a Derrida, lead with Foucault and follow up with a Kristeva.

Yet, as is well known, there are certain French wines of the finest kind that do not travel well; my wife, indeed, also of the finest kind, suffers from much the same problem. And so the wisdom resident in Paris is not necessarily the same as that in the wider – which from the French point of view is the narrower – world beyond, and what is exported is not necessarily Structuralism entire. Hence, as Frank Kermode was pointing out only the

17

other day in a major review (or was it down the snug at the Star and Garter, I cannot remember), we are faced with an anomaly. For the works that have been translated are not *all* the works we have; the names we know are not all the names we need to know; and the reputations that are *au courant* in the United States and even Britain are not all the reputations. And when Kermode was challenged, as he often is, to give an example, he quickly cited, if I remember correctly, a striking instance: the caseless case, the nameless name, of Henri Mensonge.

In this matter as in so many he was perfectly right. For if, as some of us serious scholars frequently do, you were to give up your Christmas festivities and the sight of your happy loved ones and travel, as scholars must, to America to attend the annual December conference of the Modern Language Association, where twelve thousand or so distinguished literary academics gather to discuss the work of a much smaller number of great authors, while the graduate students carry their suitcases up to their rooms and perform other small favours in the hope of an appointment to the faculty, you would come away with the same impression – as well as a large number of publishers' inspection copies of heavy course books you are never likely to look at again. This is a forum where all should be discussed, the latest stir in the world of Chaucer and Langland, the hottest news on mimesis and ambiguity, the most innovative ideas in feminist revisionism and reception theory, every single ripe cherry on the bough of literary thought. Yet go along to the sessions on Deconstruction, attend the panel on, say, 'Aporia or Mis-En-Abîme? Derrida and the "Learned Sock" of Walter Benjamin', and raise at the end a question about the work of Mensonge, and you would doubtless get a dusty answer and afterwards be left drinking all on your own at the Lesbian Linguistics Cash Bar.

Similarly go into any good bookstore, if you can find one, and flip through the pages of any or all of the now innumerable volumes of Structuralist-Deconstructionist classnotes and breviaries on offer, and it is a fair guess that nowhere will you find glimpse or glimmer of Mensonge's name. A brief survey across my own library shelves confirms the point. Thus, inspecting the capacious index of John Sturrock's fine and useful collection of essays called *Structuralism and Since* (1979), I see it moves promptly from 'Meaninglessness' to 'Metaphor' without even naming 'Mensonge'. Terence Hawkes's notable *Structuralism and Semiotics* (1977) passes grandly from McCabe and McLuhan to metaphor and metonymy with similar insouciance, though to be frank Hawkes, who has written a little in the Mensonge field, should have known better. Its companion volume, Christopher Norris's *Deconstruction: Theory and Practice* (1982), likewise freely romps from Matisse to Mehlman and Merleau-Ponty, and Vincent B. Leitch's *Deconstructive Criticism* (1983) from Mehlman to Merwin, without even noticing the gap, or as they would doubtless prefer to call it the aporia. Go, for that matter, out on to any campus and detain a group of today's finest and freshest students, as they step bright and greenhaired out to their classes on creative misprision and feminist deixis, and confront them with the word Mensonge. You would undoubtedly get some very blank stares and, such is the anxiety about sexual harassment in the academic groves these days, probably a spray of Mace in the eyes as well.

How then are we to explain the blank faces and the blank spaces, the rupture, the fracture, the slippage, the sloppage, the total loss of signification, that marks or rather does not mark the spot where the name 'Mensonge' should stand? How do we account for the *blanching white* of the figure who, in the eyes of those who like myself have watched the entire revolutionary affair not from the outside but the inside, if an inside it has got, really *is* Structuralism and Deconstruction – the man who stands at the heart of the whole tendency, if it can be said to have a heart, who represents its entire essence, if an essence-less philosophy can in any way be thought to have an essence, who displays to us what the theory really *means*, if meaning in any fashion is what it is concerned with? No, Mensonge goes unknown, or very nearly.

Yet, to those of us who know very well we are well in the know, and are aware how this entire movement came about, Mensonge is the source and the start, unquestionably the Structuralist's Structuralist, the Deconstructor's Deconstructor. He is the hub and the nub, the core and more. Nor does his achievement stop there. He is that rare and extraordinary figure, a man who has at once been able to stand with one foot firmly planted at the very beginning of the major modern thought-movement, while with his other foot standing twenty years later at the very end of it. Indeed, if movements of this kind can be said to have a shape, from the moments of initial prefiguring, the first proairetic impulses (as we say), to the time when they begin to reach closure (*clôture*) and disappear into their own profundities (as we also say), then the shape of Structuralism and Deconstruction is surely the shapeless shape of Henri Mensonge. He could be called both the John the Baptist and the St Paul the Apostle of the entire episode; what is more, he has played the key role in the momentous events lying in between. This is the man but for whom Eco would have most certainly gone unheard, and it seems unlikely that Derrida could have been conceived without him. How then is it possible that a figure so central has lacked so much attention? How can we begin to explain the neglect in which his name is held – or rather, perhaps, not held, since almost no one one meets, and I meet quite a few, seems ever to have heard of it?

One might of course ask whether it is necessary to explain it, since we manage without worrying to neglect quite a lot of other people, and we seem to have gone on thinking perfectly well without him. Yet to that question the answer must undoubtedly be a resounding yes, for the truth is if we are really to confront Structuralism and Deconstruction with any sort of clarity, if that is what is needed, we certainly have to comprehend Mensonge's absence – and quite as much, if not more, than we do most people's presence. For Mensonge's absence is no chance or random case of a chap just not being there when you are looking for him. It is an act of faith, a matter of design, a deed of determination, indeed one might say an *ontological necessity*, or to be more precise an *anti-ontological necessity*.

In fact if we are to make sense of Deconstruction at all, and goodness knows it is a difficult enough task even on a very good day, we would be wise to begin by trying to consider Mensonge and to comprehend the *significance of his non-significance*, to read the floating nature of his signless sign. And at once we find ourselves entering the entire core of the Structuralist-Deconstructionist argument, the centre of its case. For the whole affair is nothing other than a profound modern philosophy *of*, precisely, absences. Indeed, it speaks, as Jacques Derrida has reminded us, not once but several times, to the basic error that has confused all Western thought and led us into our present difficulties, the crucial error of 'the ethic of presence, an ethic of nostalgia for origins, an ethic of archaic and natural innocence, of purity of presence and self-presence in speech' which has persistently disabled us until Deconstruction happened to come along and was able to set us all right again, as we now are today.

The undermining of the illusion of presence indeed goes back to the early days of the tendency, and was famously developed by Roland Barthes in his great essay of 1968 on the Death of the Author, 'La Mort de l'auteur' – an essay of some moment here, because its writing coincides roughly with the time when our problems with Mensonge began. What Barthes in that fine brief piece was able to prove, conclusively and to most of our satisfactions, was that the literary Author – the kind of author who goes around signing copies, claiming authority and wisdom for the books he likes to think he wrote, and suggesting indeed that he has accurately presented 'reality' (never a good word to use these days) – is really an invention of bourgeois mercantile capitalism, probably only devised to let us find and buy the volumes in the bookstores without actually having to open every one up to try to discover who they were not by. For what Barthes asserted was indeed that they were not by anyone at all, or certainly not by their authors; for writers do not write but get written, and by *something outside themselves*. Of course we know this from experience; often it is a wife, an old aunt, the bank-manager, one's literary agent, or some new girl at the publishers who, unable to make head or tale of the stuff, sits down and rewrites it all completely for clarity. Barthes, however, argues more daringly that the responsible party is not another person at all, not being in favour of the concept. What writes books is in fact nothing other than history, culture, or to be more precise *language itself*. Indeed so effective is language that it has frequently arrived early in the morning, sat down at the typewriter, and as good as completed half a day's work before the average so-called author has even showered, dressed and got through his breakfast *croissant*.

Barthes's effective dispatching of the Author must be counted one of the greatest achievements of early Structuralism, and things have certainly not been the same since. As he complained: 'The Author is a modern figure, a product of our society insofar as, emerging from the Middle Ages with English empiricism, French rationalism and the personal faith of the Reformation, it discovered *the prestige of the individual*, or, as it is more nobly put, the "human person . . ."' (my italics, or more probably writing's). It is this that has given us the writer as tyrant, the author as false authority, the self-flattering figure who is attracting all the attention that should fairly be going elsewhere – to the Structuralist critic, for example. 'The *author*', Barthes asserted (not my italics, though I am not sure whose), 'still reigns in histories of literature, biographies of writers, interviews, magazines, as in the very consciousness of men of letters anxious to unite their person and their work through diaries and memoirs.' Compelled to correct this delusory emphasis, Barthes replaced the writer with writing, and his text with the reader: 'the text's unity lies not in its origin but its destination,' he declared, and as he said of the book, 'no one, no "person" says it; its source, its voice, is not the true place of the writing, which is reading.'

This obviously touched many chords, and Barthes's argument was rapidly acclaimed. It was particularly popular with publishers, who quickly realized that, if you said that authors wrote books, you had to pay them, whereas if you claimed that readers did, they had the habit of paying you, a much more effective commercial arrangement. It also had considerable appeal for British critics, who had always taken the view that all authors were dead anyway, or if they were not then they should be. There was therefore little wonder that Barthes's book achieved massive sales. Unfortunately because of the nature of its argument he was unable to claim the royalties, and since he was living by writing at the time he soon found himself in difficulties. It was rumoured here and there that he could be seen begging in the gutters and the tunnels of the Metro, but this was never confirmed. What was certainly clear was that he had achieved what he set out to do. As he said, 'we know that to give writing its future, it is necessary to overthrow the myth: the birth of the reader must be at the cost of the death of the Author.' Barthes died in 1980.

Barthes's powerful argument ('What can no longer be spoken is the proper noun') had enormous influence on further thinking in the field. For it soon became clear that if it was possible to deconstruct the author as a person the same argument ought to work with anyone, or indeed everyone. The decisive implications of this were developed by Michel Foucault, who was shortly able to prove that we all of us lived in the age of the total *disappearance of the subject*. As he put it, 'The researches of psycho-analysis, of linguistics, of anthropology have "decentred" the subject in relation to the laws of its desire, the forms of language, the rules of its actions, or the play of its mythical and imaginative discourse.' The disappearance of the subject was another enormous step, of considerable relevance to the fate of Mensonge. But these were still the early days of the argument, which was further refined by the Deconstructionist Jacques Derrida, who was able to demonstrate with a totally convincing philosophical obscurity that all concepts of 'presence', 'identity', 'self' and the like were fabrications, desperate attempts to retain the attached signifier when it had departed long ago.

In a series of bold transverse moves, Derrida had soon demolished the entire heresy of the proper noun, showing that the names we signed on cheques were not our own or anyone else's either, and eliminating the metaphysics of *all* forms of presence under any pretext whatsoever. All that was left was a persistent *deferral* of identity, a kind of foreplay to existence without the satisfaction of an outcome, apparently increasingly popular in France. It had now been made clear that everything had been deconstructed, and that the proper noun, the author, the self, the book, the object, the reader, the referent, the real, were all floating items of signification without a base. This bold sequence of philosophical developments made for clarity and brought us to where we are today, wherever that may be.

It did, however, make for certain problems, the problems indeed that were to be so boldly confronted, or so we think, by Henri Mensonge. Thus, if the author was dead, it was still necessary to have a Deconstructionist author who could explain this to us. Though the book was dead, someone or something had to explain this in the Deconstructionist book. The subject might be proven subjectless, but it was necessary for somebody, or some body, to prove this to us. Thus Deconstruction had to establish an authority that was beyond authority, an interpretation that was beyond interpretation, a presence that was beyond absence, a non-transcendental transcendental beyond the grave. And it is here, and now, that we see the significance of the non-significance of Henri Mensonge.

The fact is that Deconstruction itself was based on an illogicality Mensonge was determined to refute. And it is thus we can say that his non-presence is exactly what constitutes his authority, or rather, precisely, his lack of it. This is the position he has chosen to make clear, or as clear as he can in the circumstances of his not being there. So, as he was to declare in an unsigned essay we take to be by him, or by some other anonymous person speaking in his name: 'You must understand that the "fact" of my existence would negate what my text *as text* is saying. For this reason I ask you never to think of me, except perhaps at Christmas. For has it not been inevitable that, having written as "I" have "written", having thought as "I" have "thought", I should then refuse to be "here", or "there", or "anywhere else" for that matter?' Or, as he reverts to the matter in another text we take, with equally little evidence, to be by him: 'Let it be enough that you have the good fortune to have a text to read. Do not ask that there be an "I" who wrote it. For if there were an "I", it could not be an "it", for it would reconstruct that metaphysics of presence "it" has determined to destroy. Thus we would have wasted a good deal of time I am sure both of us, or neither, could have spent in far better ways.'

To sum up, Mensonge is not absent solely for himself, as a more selfish absentee might choose to be. Indeed his non-presence is evidence of a profound philosophical heroism. Would we could say the same of his later disciples who, in the same logical crisis, have sought to evade the problem by various devices of what they laughingly call a ludic kind, and who have persisted in being present even when there is no logical ground for them to be so. Indeed they are everywhere, hanging around campuses, publishing new books, turning up at parties – even though the fundamental principles of their own cognition should tell them that in the very least they should remain in the non-privacy of their own homes.

This is why we must admire and celebrate Mensonge, could we find him. For there is no doubt at all that, had he wished or found it logical, he could have claimed all the modern rewards of his outstanding achievement. In an age that delights in celebrating celebrity, endlessly desires to recognize recognition, and acclaim success as a great success, Mensonge could everywhere have become MENSONGE, satisfying the dreams and the desires of those who would have heard of his having been heard of, had he been. He could certainly have been a well-known world figure, had he simply cared to pick up from the travel-agents the many plane-tickets ordered in his name, or some-one's. He could surely have had the chair of a distinguished professor at Yale University, if he had just answered his letters, or even bothered to pick up the telephone when it rang. He could have been a regular guest on every talk-show, disputing with Austin and challenging Frege in front of audiences of several millions. But *he chose not to*.

In this of course we know that he has not been alone. Many of our greatest figures have chosen to hide away from the voracious glare of publicity and the public. Leading writers have refused to let the fiction of their work intrude on to the more complex fiction of their lives. Many have chosen an aesthetic of silence, for a variety of reasons, ranging from escape from arrest or random paternity suits to the very highest artistic principles. B. Traven hid behind a pseudonym, disappeared into Mexico, and only occasionally showed himself under another name when he was required as an extra in the films of his novels, so leaving us with a mystery inside an enigma. J. D. Salinger followed his fragile heroes and heroines into silence, departing his 'distinctly Manhattanesque locale' for residence behind a fence in New

Hampshire so high we have no idea whether or not he may be on the other side of it today. Samuel Beckett did, it is true, permit a biography to be written, but only on the strict condition that he was not in it. Thomas Pynchon exists in only one photograph, which some people think is actually J. D. Salinger, and when he is summoned to receive the literary honours won by his abstruse and elusive fictions it is a clown who arrives to collect them – a device that also seems to be increasingly used in political life. And the French writer Jean Genet, in his later years, refused to give his publishers his address or his name, and was said to collect his royalties, reputedly very substantial, from a hollow tree somewhere in the Bois de Boulogne by dead of night.

Yet even in these cases we recognize *a something that hides itself*, an *absent presence*. Mensonge has gone further, insisting that he was never even there in the first place, has never been known to anyone, even his closest friends, that he is no one, has achieved nothing, and does not exist. In short he has claimed to be a totally *absent absence*. 'I have sought a level of absence that is so complete it *cannot be mistaken for anything other than it is*,' he, or whoever, has explained. We know that absence teases, constructs an enigma, plays a ludic game of seduction and stimulates curiosity and desire. Mensonge has had no part even in that. 'Unlike my philosophical colleagues, those Don Giovannis of modern thought,' 'he' says, 'I have chosen to generate no desire, excite no sense of pleasure, exercise no seduction, and when the crucial moment of *jouissance* arises, if it ever does, you will discover that I am *nowhere to be found*.'

We can imagine that this has not been easy for him, and indeed we can find in 'his' writings a glimpse or two of what it has cost. 'Yes, I have refused to seduce,' he says. 'Think what a sacrifice this is for anyone who is, or might be, a Frenchman. Yet I remember how much worse it would be to sacrifice an even more important Gallic prize – one's *logicality*.' To this commitment Mensonge has remained steadfastly faithful. For instance, in recent years he has insisted that his name should not appear anywhere in print, on the spines or title pages of books, whether they are by him or not, which we shall never know anyway. 'Think of me as the *deus absconditus* who could very well *never*

26

*have created a universe in the first place,*' he is reported to have remarked, through a train window, to some acquaintance. In that strange comment, for which we have only very dubious authority, we undoubtedly get the full flavour of Henri Mensonge.

Mensonge may be considered our truest, our most necessary, philosopher, the ultimate case of Deconstructionist *integrity* – the man who has out-Barthesed Barthes, out-Foucaulted Foucault, out-Derridaed Derrida, out-Deleuzed-and-Guattaried Deleuze and Guattari. At the same time it must be admitted from the point of view of serious scholarship that his honest stance has left us with some very considerable difficulties. For, if we are to *prove* his absence, and make his point for him, we need some evidence of his original existence, if only so that we can be sure that it is he who has disappeared, and not some complete impostor. 'I have done all I can, in the age when the proper noun is dead, to eliminate that far too proper noun "Mensonge" completely from the world,' he is supposed to have said, 'even up to the point of not writing the things that keep on being attributed to him, or me.' This increases the problem. For, while we must respect his wish to be, as he puts it, 'a totally floating signifier, drifting away downstream, or up, according to how my lack of desire takes me', we have reached a scholarly impasse where, in order to identify his contribution, construct his bibliography, and also send on his mail (which, incidentally, contains many unpaid bills, some very substantial) we need to establish his not being there *authoritatively*. But, for the time being, he remains the purest instance we have of *la mort de l'auteur*, living, we think, proof of Roland Barthes's famous comment that 'Linguistically, the Author is never more than the instance writing.' Yet even Barthes, who did so much to lead us into the impasse in which we now find ourselves, did not alas explain just how to deal with the problems that arise when we can find no Author at all to deconstruct.

Of course, and inevitably, the quest for Mensonge has begun, and it is bound to continue, though it will not be easy. If the history of modern philosophy is to be written, we have to fill in the space he has opened for us. If we are to understand the crisis of our thought, we need to know what questions he refuses to answer. Because he has chosen to be nowhere, we are likely to find him everywhere. He has become the trace of an existence that chooses to leave no trace, and scholarship requires that we follow the lead he so steadfastly has refused to give us. In electing to be an enigma that will not even be enigmatic, he has puzzled and teased us that much more. By becoming the crucial silence at the heart of the busy noise of redundancy in so much postmodern discourse, he forces us to listen hard, though so far we have heard nothing, or not much. He is an absence who has shown the illusion of presence far more clearly than those who have been present to tell us about it, but we would surely like to see him plain. He has pointed to the essential task of the times, the Deconstruction of Deconstruction itself, and in that enterprise we have no better absent leader than he, if he would simply show us the way. There is no doubt at all that we cannot today avoid pursuing the significance, or otherwise, and so confronting face to face the absent absence of Henri Mensonge.

# 4

Thus it is that the strange quest for Henri Mensonge undoubtedly confronts the dedicated scholar with many remarkable and unusual problems – problems so great that, to be quite frank, a good many of my colleagues would not dream of undertaking the enterprise at all, preferring something far safer and more certain to ensure academic promotion, if there is to be any any more. Yet so great is the challenge, and so substantial the potential reward, that it would be a shame to evade it, and I do not propose to try. The first task, of course, is to establish the biography, or so it would be in the normal way. Alas, what with the Death of the Author and the Disappearance of the Subject, even an ordinary biography is bound to be a problem these days. Biographies are said to be fictions revealing more about the biographer than they do about their subjects, who of course do not exist anyway. As Barthes says: 'The image of literature to be found in ordinary culture is tyrannically centred on the author, his person, his life, his tastes, his passions . . .' and to be honest it has to be admitted that, once all these have been removed, there is not really a lot for a biographer to work on. In any case our modern authors seem to have learned most of the fine arts of eluding the modern biographer, habitually shredding their papers and swearing their friends to a secrecy that, happily, they are rarely capable of maintaining. As Emily Dickinson, no mean evader herself, once observed, 'Biography first convinces us of the fleeing of the Biographied.' It is a comment that has a peculiar appropriateness to the case of Mensonge.

Just why they should be so anxious, in a time when our

capacity to demystify and psycho-analyse them has so much increased, is not clear. Perhaps, again, Barthes has explained it: 'he is intolerant at an *image* of himself, he suffers at being named,' he wrote, in fact about himself, in a third-person work of self-biography shyly titled *Roland Barthes by Roland Barthes*. There are times when it seems that Deconstruction is a little bit *too* full of paradoxes, and one cannot but feel that enigmas are indeed there for a reason. After all, Salome did not dress in seven veils so that no one would notice her, and secrets are not hidden at the end of labyrinths in the hope that no one will ever go looking for them. There is also the curious fact that, despite our general conceptual dismissal of them, biographies sell remarkably well and often far better than the actual works of the authors in question, something not entirely to be overlooked in an era of market forces. In any case, one simply does not get a research grant for sitting down and doing nothing whatsoever, or certainly not any more in these Reaganite and Thatcherite days.

So perhaps it is not surprising that, despite all the theoretical anxieties, we are already beginning to see the first halting stages, the first trace of a trace, of what might be called the angular quest for Henri Mensonge. Indeed the time was bound to come when, given his steadfast refusal to write himself, others would come along and try to write him. The initial hints followed by anxious guesses, the tiny statements followed by sudden erasures, are beginning to be set down; and something that is just starting to resemble the sketch of a glimpse of a draft of something resembling a kind of life is stumblingly being put together. The task, of course, is inordinately difficult and the journey onward will be long. For one thing, Mensonge himself is no idiot in these matters, and has blocked the road to the best of his ability. Indeed for a long time it was regularly supposed that there simply was *no Mensonge* – that he was a hypothetical figure or a convenient fiction, invented by some teasing journalist, hack writer or complex theoretician for his or her own purposes. But this simply showed how very skilful Mensonge had been. Now we are starting to by-pass the error and set our stumbling feet on the difficult and precipitous road toward him.

Evidence has begun to accumulate – a lost credit-card here,

an unanswered letter asking for the return of a favourite sweater there – which indicates that there really is a life waiting to be discovered and unravelled, were we only able to find a research foundation or wealthy private individual willing to sponsor the enterprise at the high capital level that such an important study deserves. The task will be quite exceptional, and will need a quality of dedication rare even among the remarkable community of biographical researchers whom we find amongst us at the moment, mostly sitting over drinks in the bar at the Groucho. But this is a story so central to our times that we cannot evade it. It will require subtlety of thought, psychological insight, an instinct for deception. It promises surprises, laughter, and a considerable air of mystery, with characters of postmodern elusiveness and good foreign locations. I think there can be very little doubt it is worth going on with, and as soon as possible, before what evidence there is disappears. Indeed I have my bags packed already.

But let us begin by asking just what, in our present state of unknowing, do we know so far about the mysterious Mensonge? It is not a great deal. First, it would appear that this exemplary French intellectual was not by birth French at all. The scrappy evidence so far suggests he was born in Bulgaria during the last or some other war, left his native land as a result of some quarrel or other, said to be about an umbrella, and came to Paris only because of a confusion about trains. Here he appears to have attended a French *lycée*, though the school that has a name resembling his on its rolls also marks him persistently absent, the child evidently being father of the man. He then, it seems, proceeded to the prestigious Ecole des Gens Supérieurs – that remarkable French forcing-house from which so many of the heroes, and some of the heroines, of French intellectual, literary, artistic, ministerial, scientific and culinary life have been drawn – to study for the *baccalauréat*, and the record suggests he did well, indeed attaining a speed of well over 50 w.p.m.

Certainly the laurels must have come his way, for he thereafter appears to have procceded to the even more prestigious Ecole Pratique des Grandes Hautes Etudes, where he must have worked with that great scourge of traditionalist French criticism, none other than the still more prestigious Roland Barthes. It is said he worked with him for a time on road signs, until at last the subject became virtually obliterated in the rush to study it. Nonetheless Barthes's *sémanalyse* clearly pointed him in the right direction and got him on to the correct road. Mensonge had now doubtless got his grounding in Structuralism, and was probably also guided by Barthes in his decision to lead a marginal intellectual existence, much in fashion in those days. Mensonge thus appears to have supported himself, if exigently, by journalism, fire-eating, and acting as travel guide to Japanese tourists visiting the Eiffel Tower during the summer. And it was probably also thanks to Barthes's assistance that he now joined the remarkable group of new critics who were working for and around surely the best French periodical of the time, the famous magazine *Quel Tel* – to which he contributed articles and reviews of film, television and traffic accidents, writing under one if not several pseudonyms.

What, then, was his position? Like most French intellectuals of that date, Mensonge appears to have had strong and committed political interests. Indeed he would seem to have been a Marxist, though he disagreed with Karl Marx over several things, including the withering away of the state and the exact dating of the eighteenth brumaire. He was, after all, living in a time of new radical adventure, when the young guard were determined to challenge the old in every possible way. Indeed at this time Mensonge appears to have got into several fights in homes for the aged, and spent two or three nights in jail. This all culminated of course in the great *événements* of May 1968, when the younger generation erupted in various colourful spots all over the world, and a new utopia seemed to be in process of birth, especially in Paris. Evidently Mensonge was involved, and we hear of him over this period on the streets with his peers, carrying various small rocks and banners of such intellectual subtlety and oblique demand that few if any could understand them. The Structuralist-Deconstructionist had clearly been born. In the period of intellectual disappointment and defeat which followed, it became clear that utopia was not going to arrive immediately, and might well keep everyone waiting for several more years, and might take a good deal of hard labour.

Certainly this was a time when Mensonge's life appears to have changed considerably. For some time he had been teaching in various schools and universities, even at times at the invitation of the institution concerned. When the Sorbonne was, largely for political reasons, divided into a number of smaller and diversified campuses, such as Vincennes and Nanterre, Mensonge apparently found employment at one of the lesser-known of these, Paris XIV, in Banlieue Seine-et-Loire, a very slow commute from Montparnasse, and actually a good deal more convenient to Hamburg. He seems here, perhaps surprisingly, to have taught classics; however, we must assume he liked it, since the academic records show he applied in the early 1970s for the Chair of Complicated Thinking in the Department of Philosophy. He was, alas, turned down on a technicality, not being what they were looking for, which was a woman. If, as we surmise, he was also a foreigner, this too would have told against him, chairs in French universities normally going only to nationals or their very closest relations.

Thereafter, in a country where paper is important, Mensonge seems to have been written down on remarkably little of it. Official records show no trace at all of his residence or his activities. Indeed, and perhaps partly as a result of his academic disappointments, we here enter the period of his greatest, and also most famous, obscurity. And this is about all we have in the way of a documentary history of the man. We can only acknowledge that it is little more than a start, a mite better than nothing. For anything more we must step beyond biography and look to the writings themselves, if, that is, we can find them.

# 5

The controversy over what and what not Mensonge has written persists to this day, and will no doubt continue. The most refined skills of the bibliographer and the plodding doggedness of the relentless pedant are necessary to distinguish the small witty reviews, the quarrelling and abusive asides, the political polemics and the cultural commentaries that are scattered through the pages of *Quel Tel* and other ephemera and are often thought to be in his style, but there can still be no complete confidence about these attributions. However, the key fact is this. Over the early years of the 1960s, when Mensonge was often thought to be drifting, he was by no means idling away his time. Indeed, working totally alone, he was busy conceiving, gestating, nurturing, nearly bringing to birth, and then recalling, reconceiving, reconstructing, rewriting, cutting up into small pieces, reordering and then parenting his one, and very possibly his only, masterwork.

It is the one book that bears his authoritative signature, the book we know him by. It came out in 1965, or just possibly 1966. The date, whichever it is, is crucial. For this means that it appeared certainly one year, and very possibly even two, *before*, and therefore not *after*, the key Deconstructionist year of 1967. We call it that because this was the year in which Mensonge's strongest rival, Jacques Derrida, imposed himself on the intellectual scene, not with just one brilliant book but with three (*Of Grammatology*, *Writing and Difference*, and *Speech and Phenomena*), and very possibly the annual revision of the Michelin Guide as well. So a new spirit was clearly passing through Parisian thought, and it is usually from Derrida's year that the entire development of the Post-Structuralist or Deconstructionist enterprise is usually dated. However we – I and now you – know quite differently. For Mensonge's book – it was called *La Fornication comme acte culturel* – came first. And so potent was its argument, so radical its impact, that it does indeed seem perfectly correct to say that Derrida could not have been conceived without the assistance of Mensonge.

Yet it is typical of the man that even here there are great obscurities. Mensonge's book turned into a chapter of accidents, or an accident of chapters. Clearly it should have taken Paris by storm, exactly as Derrida's did. However, *La Fornication* – to give the work its usual short title – had, to put it at its least, a strange and unusual publishing history. Mensonge – who appears to have been as confused in his personal life as he is clear-minded in his writings – seemingly failed to appreciate the universal French convention that any book that is not actually published in Paris is considered not to exist, is certainly not to be talked about, and at best is to be regarded as a mistake. Mensonge would certainly have had no difficulty at all in finding a leading Parisian publisher. But perhaps with characteristic elusiveness, or perhaps foolishly – and as a result, it has been claimed, of some brief but presumably tempestuous *liaison* about which we have nonetheless been able to find out little, if not nothing – he was tempted into submitting his extraordinary manuscript somewhere else. The outlet he chose – the Imprimerie Kouskous in the Rue des Timbres-Postes, in the small duchy of Luxembourg – is not a well-known house, and indeed it subsequently proved to be a very ineffective cover for the international drugs trade. Here, whether because of incompetence, indifference, or the natural difficulty of obtaining an adequate supply of paper in what is quite a small duchy, only a very limited number of copies of the work were printed.

Nor was the process done well. Innumerable errors were introduced, unless Mensonge had put them there already, the typestyle is inconsistent, and most copies are on a porous paper of a kind conventionally used for purposes quite other than literary and philosophical dissemination. Distribution was no better managed, and the book went on sale only in a small number of Parisian bookstores, mostly of the sort described as 'unusual'. Perhaps the title was misleading; certainly it ended up in the kind of bookstore specializing in erotica and in genital technology of the more complicated kind, or else in those serving the always large Eastern European *émigré* population of the city – the community of which Mensonge was presumably a member, though one must doubt if he ever turned up at its meetings. Even so, despite all these disadvantages, the book soon established a reputation among the *cognoscenti* for its radical philosophical import. Indeed it was soon hardly possible to walk past the café terraces of Montparnasse without overhearing the leading French intellectuals engaging in a constant intense discussion of *La Fornication*.

The stir of discussion was slowly to place Mensonge not quite at the centre of French intellectual thought, for though he walked about a good deal he could never find it, but certainly somewhere close by. And this is why we can justly surmise that all those great Deconstructionist events that were soon to follow, all those radical new achievements that marked the second stage of the Structuralist revolution, all the strange new positions that were being taken up, were a direct result of *La Fornication*. Yet, characteristically, Mensonge did nothing to capitalize on the newly-won fame that is rightly due to a radical new figure in the forefront of French philosophy. He did not, as far as we know, buy a sports car. He neither met nor had any knowable relationship of any kind with Brigitte Bardot. He did not appear on French cultural television endlessly discussing architecture. He was seen with no notable mistresses, and appeared in none of the leading intellectual restaurants, not even just for coffee afterwards. He was never even spotted in a *bôite*. He was not made Minister of Culture. His life changed, as far as we know, remarkably little, except, of course, to be far less *there* than before. He seems to have continued his obscure teaching of the classics, making no notable impact. Students who took his courses at Paris XIV at the close of the 1960s testify that they had no idea that the course they were taking on Aristotle's *Anorexics* was taught to them by the great Mensonge – in part because he rarely appeared, and a small boy on a bicycle came by with copious notes which were distributed gratis to the class, and proved useless in the subsequent examinations, so almost all of them have been thrown away.

Little more is known. When intellectual journalists attempted to contact him, they discovered that the telephone had not only been disconnected but wrenched completely off the wall by some blunt instrument. Landladies at the addresses he sometimes gave professed no knowledge of him, or anyone else for that matter, perhaps a wise move in a Paris always hospitable to foreign guest-workers except at certain times of the year. Young scholars desperately wanting to sit at his feet could find no trace whatever of the feet at which they wished to sit, though one pair of shoes was subsequently retrieved from the cobbler's and is now in the Pompidou Centre, with 45 francs still owing on the repair. Occasionally in some journal devoted to the growing industry in semiotics an article said to be by Mensonge would appear, stimulating sudden sales and renewed curiosity about his existence, or lack of it. His reputation spread abroad, though very selectively. Some specialist American scholars grew interested, and began coming specially to Paris in the hope of making contact with the major new force in Deconstructive thinking. In the early 1970s they could be seen in considerable numbers sitting in a variety of restaurants opposite an empty chair, looking at their watches and checking with waiters who denied all knowledge of any booking for that evening, though of course that is what waiters are wont to do.

And that, for now, is it. The record of the facts, or what used to be called the facts, really needs constructing afresh, and from the very beginning. All traces remain obscure. And what of the man himself, his appearance and his character? His students and the odd mistress so far consulted profess to remember nothing at all about him, except a faint whiff of Bulgarian tobacco and some unclean personal habits. Until lately, only two photographs appear to exist; both have since disappeared, and neither can be taken as definitive. In one he sits, a handsome, dark-eyed if decidedly portly young man, of somewhat Slavic appearance, at a table on the terrace of what may or may not be the Café des

Deux Magots. The date is quite indeterminate, the prevailing *chic* of figures in the background suggesting either the 1950s or the 1980s. A bock is on the table in front of him, next to the usual saucer, which he appears to have filled with some liquid. There is also what seems to be a female shoe; it has been argued that this could signify something, though knowing Mensonge as we do, or do not, probably it does not. One arm is raised high at the shoulder, perhaps in a form of revolutionary salute, more probably in a gesture of rage toward the photographer.

The other photograph, presumably taken some years later, or else much earlier, shows him now quite fat, balding, and several inches shorter. One of his eyes now shows a marked steer to the left. He stands for no good reason in front of a small wooden shed, which so far no one has succeeded in identifying. He holds up a spade, and is looking at it inquiringly, though whether to dig with it, name it or strike someone with it we have no way of knowing. Neither photograph does justice to him, or anyone else for that matter; certainly it reveals nothing about his personality or character, except perhaps that it is protean. Much more recently, a third photograph has come, as it were, to light and is reproduced as the frontispiece of this book. Signed on the back with a scrawl that is putatively Mensonge's own, it appears to have been taken from the rear, though this is not certain. This makes identification difficult even for those who knew the man well, could we but find any. A dome-like and balding skull leans slightly forward to peer through curtains at some distant sight, probably the *terrasse* of the Café Flore. On the other hand, it could equally well be the passport photograph of a very retiring man.

Beyond this the record is virtually blank. No press-interviews exist in any of the conventional journals. Published analytical study of his work is curiously missing, perhaps conditioned by the fear that none of it may be by him at all. There is, of course, no autobiography. However, a book called *Non-Mensonge par Non-Mensonge* is rumoured to exist, though in manuscript only, whoever has or has not written it refusing apparently to permit its publication.

This, then, is the sum of the devastating honesty of Henri

Mensonge – a man who has refused to exist as anything more or other than a text, and perhaps not even that. Yet the fact remains that whether or not he exists we cannot do without him. He has, quite simply, become *inescapable*. For anyone concerned with the current state of thought, and our contemporary philosophical dilemma, he must be found, and quickly. His book, or perhaps rather essay (at 39 pages it is, like so many major French contributions to the history of human thought, little more than that), remains to this day the precious classic it always was. What few over-used and well-smudged copies remain from that first printing from the Imprimerie Kouskous are now collectors' items, nearly all of them held in private hands and kept in vaults under lock and key. Any surviving copies are desperately hunted, and from time to time one may be discovered on one of those small bookstalls that overhang the Seine on the remoter Paris *quais*, or more probably in the window of Basil Blackwell's. Alas, due to the extraordinary contractual arrangements Mensonge originally made with the Imprimerie Kouskous, which, since the raid of 1978, is no longer still in formal existence, but retains all the rights, along with Mensonge's overcoat, it has been impossible to reprint the text, or any other by this elusive non-author. This explains why it has never been found in any of those attractive series in which, at quite remarkable prices, most of the Structuralist and Deconstructionist texts appear. For similar reasons no part of the book has ever been anthologized, and is very rarely quoted; the publishers of the present volume acknowledge they are taking the most extraordinary risks in providing in these pages Mensongian materials which have simply never been seen before in print.

The same complicated contractual arrangements undoubtedly explain why it is that there has been no English-language translation of *La Fornication*. There are at last rumours that it is being attempted, and will appear in due time from the West Coast Marxist-Feminist Gay Collective Press, under the title *Sex and Culture*, with a lovely cover, in their 'His-and-Her-Meneutics' series. But for the present moment, a few worn copies of this ill-printed and ill-starred book must remain the obscure repository of one of the most potent and important statements of modern thinking we have had. We may consider them as, in their way, quite as precious and quite as potential as the famous Shakespeare and Company edition of James Joyce's *Ulysses* was during the 1920s, when that momentous book was banned by the customs and postal authorities in both the United States and Britain, and was habitually burned when discovered amid the underwear of the hungry young intellectuals who so quickly realized its importance and its value. Today, of course, Joyce's book is widely recognized as a universal classic, and of it too we might say that Deconstruction could not exist without it. It has, of course, become a world-wide bestseller, everywhere bought even though perhaps not always everywhere read. It does not seem too much to propose that, in a few years' time – when the contractual problems are resolved, the place of this great philosopher made quite clear, the quest for Mensonge completed, the mystery solved – *La Fornication* will enjoy a similar happy fate.

# 6

Of the importance of *La Fornication* there is simply no doubt. But just what was the *nature* of Henri Mensonge's extraordinary intervention in the amazing philosophical revolution of our time? Here is the question that begs for its answer; but we will not fully understand the scale of the achievement unless we go back, just for a moment, to the city of Paris in those strange, bleak yet heady years right after the Liberation and the close of the Second World War, and the philosophical crisis it engendered. For these were, philosophically, troubled times. France had been an occupied land, and the German Occupation divided French intellectuals as they had rarely been divided before, certainly not since the first performance of Stravinsky's *Rite of Spring*. Some had, it must be admitted, been collaborators, active or passive supporters of the Nazi invaders. Others had heroically fought in or assisted the Resistance. Yet others had accepted the responsibility for remaining at their desks and preserving that crucial modern heritage of Kierkegaardian Fear-and-Trembling and Heideggerian *angst* which the Third Reich so ruthlessly set out to destroy. Rarely before had the relation between thought and action been so severely tested; today in the comfortable if troubled Western world we can scarcely recapture what this actually meant, though attempting to put together a do-it-yourself pine room divider from the instructions provided by its Finnish manufacturer might give a very faint and fragile clue to the feeling of crisis. Never before had philosophy mattered so much, becoming an issue not only of the Nice and the True but of ultimate acceptance of duty and responsibility.

41

Small wonder, then, that these immediate postwar years were a bitter, contentious sort of time, and that when the cafés and restaurants began slowly to refill with intellectuals returning to pick up their philosophical duties the tables began to resound with cries of *trahison des clercs* and *mauvaise foi*, whether with or without the *crevettes*. What Albert Camus so powerfully described, when he too popped in, as 'Hitler's nihilist revolution' had sharpened the deep belief in absurdity that thinkers had been experimenting with for much of the century. The atomic age had begun, Marshall Aid had started, and nothing made very much sense. Rebellion was in the air, Plight and Alienation were universal, and the black beret made its welcome appearance. To all the serious young minds, as they gathered of an evening over the newly fashionable espresso coffee and surveyed the ruins of the world, it was very clear that the famous question Heidegger had posed to the twentieth century – 'Why is there any being at all and not rather nothing?' – required an immediate answer, or at the very least an urgent holding letter. These were new times, and this was the question the postwar intelligentsia, faced with a history of modern crisis, had to sit down somewhere and try to solve. And indeed they did, attempting a variety of answers, some on the backs of postcards, some in the form of major books which were seized on throughout the West, as the universal symptoms of postwar alienation and anomie spread like non-specific urethritis.

Of the many answers, there can be no doubt that the most complete and compelling came from the strange charismatic figure of Jean-Paul Sartre, the prophet of postwar Existentialism. Existentialism was not itself new, and indeed Sartre himself had been examining absurdity in considerable depth even before the war started. But recent experiences had concentrated his mind wonderfully, especially as far as the work on Nothingness was concerned. Sartre, who had been heroic in the Resistance, was thus well prepared to make it absolutely clear to everyone that we all live in a state of nausea, in a godless and forsaken universe of viscous contingency and random thinginess, condemned to be born, live in hell, which was mostly other people, and then condemned to die, none of this for any good reason that anyone could come up with. This coincided with the experience of most people condemned to be living at the time, especially when they got up with not too good a head of a Sunday morning. Thus was the great movement of postwar Sartrean Existentialism brought to birth, and there was scarcely a young thinker of the late 1940s or early 1950s who was not prepared to agree that the world was self-evidently absurd, or certainly silly in some pretty obvious way, and that we all lived in a state of contingency and alienation – unable to define ourselves, anyone else, or even reach an adequate decision about what we wanted for breakfast. Youthful rebels appeared in all the major Western cities, most of them writing plays for the Royal Court Theatre, arguing that existence felt inauthentic and it was impossible to experience true sensations, especially if you lived in Stoke.

Gloom may have spread everywhere, but the youthful new rebels were not without style. They crowded everywhere in their berets and black stockings, gathered in the new espresso bars where the coffee machines worked without steam and the intellectuals steamed without working, listening to records by Juliette Greco, mocking the passing bourgeoisie, and discoursing on the general senselessness of life. The girls all wore existentialist black, and the fellows were all strange clones of Marlon Brando, raising the suspicion that he had conducted some concealed European tour during the mid-1930s and left issue behind. Wherever one went, if one saw any point in going anywhere, which in those days one usually did not, the endless plaint of Greco, singing of faithlessness, neglect and utter despair, sounded from the speakers while everyone chatted of *angoisse* and *le néant*. They were good times on the whole, and one cannot help wishing they would come back.

Moreover Existentialism, though sometimes misunderstood, was by no means a philosophy of total nihilism, and I think most of those involved enjoyed it. It was, after all, Sartre's point that humanism was recoverable, if not quite yet. By watching waiters at work, and examining men condemned to death for no good reason, he had come to the conclusion that Being-In-The-World was available to us, provided we did not rush it or try to take it to excess. Nausea and bad faith may be epidemic, but they could be overcome, if one willed to act and chose to become *engagé*, or at least looked for a nice girl in black and started dating regularly. Certainly existence now preceded essence, and not, as before the war, the other way round. But essence was available, if heavily rationed. Significant choice was possible, provided that one realized that one made one's choices not solely for oneself but for all others as well. Sartre acknowledged that this was difficult, as in his famous philosophical example of the man in the restaurant who has chosen fish and then cannot remember whether everyone else in the world drinks white wine or not. Yet full Being was available, and Sartre showed that it was possible to recover, if not Reality itself, then something quite closely resembling it, if in a different shade.

This, then, was the Paris that Mensonge would have known and wandered in had he arrived there at this heady and vital time. We now rather think, knowing his incorrigibly careless travel habits, that he did not, whenever he may have set off. However, *had* he been in the city at this time, as with a little more care he could have been, he would most certainly have encountered Jean-Paul Sartre and his constant and remarkable companion Simone de Beauvoir as they made their round of the cafés where the disciples gathered, she leaning on his arm or he on hers, depending on the time of day. No doubt he would also have encountered Sartre's comrade-in-arms and sometime adversary Albert Camus, as he sat on the terraces or the rear verandahs of the snout-nosed Parisian buses and discussed with his disciples (there were many disciples in those days) the myth of Sisyphus, at first thought to be a serious sexual disease but quickly seen as a profound human parable about how we all live by pushing rocks up slopes. If he had had a few francs in his pocket, he would undoubtedly have gone to the theatre and seen Samuel Beckett's *clochards*, sitting under dead trees or in dustbins and waiting, along with the audience, for something to happen. If he had not, he would undoubtedly have walked along the *quais* or in the subways of the Métro and seen someone else's *clochards* doing the same for free. Or he might have sat down with Beckett's famous trilogy of novels, reading of characters who absent themselves and turn eventually into simple pings and pongs, something he was in effect to do himself. He would certainly have become aware of the modern vision of man as a godless benighted creature wandering forlornly through an abandoned universe looking for an exit that someone has just locked a few moments before, or else as a world where, shut in some cell or white room, we attempt to describe the minute and minimal fragments of our little existence on papers which are taken away each night and never seen again, which is certainly what happens to me most of the time. He would have seen the crucial importance of modern philosophy, and also its major difficulty – which is that while serious thought usually has an erotic effect on the opposite sex, by the time it has you are normally trapped in an epistemological crisis so overwhelming you are unable to take advantage of the opportunity.

What an intellectual forcing-house Mensonge would have encountered, then, had he arrived in Paris in the late 1940s, when everything was happening. Alas, we think he probably managed to turn up about eight or ten years later, by which time the atmosphere had changed completely. By this date, the middle of the 1950s, Existentialism was done with, already giving way to Post-Existentialist ways of thought. These distrusted Sartre's optimism and humanism and dealt with the human condition in a quite new way, by suggesting that there was not one. Heroically, as usual, the writers led the way. By the early 1950s the new mood had made its mark with the *nouveau roman* – which, we should recall, arrived a little before the *nouvelle vague*, a good bit before the *nouvelle critique*, decidedly before the *nouvelle cuisine*, and at least a decade ahead of the *nouveau Beaujolais*. The novel of Robbe-Grillet, Butor, Sarraute and others disputed the whole tradition of realism, showing it to be an invention of people who thought there was something out there. It rejected the tragic humanism of Sartre and Camus, declaring that the novel was about neither tragedy nor humanism but simply presented, as Robbe-Grillet said, 'the smooth, meaningless, mindless, amoral surface of the world'. This meant that novels were made up of things – *choses*, as they were then called – which simply stood there glowering at us all the time, though there was no us, since the new novel rejected the heresy of interiority. Indeed novels could no longer have 'characters' who thought and made sense of things. These had to be replaced by pieces of furniture and small dead insects who took the responsibility for the action, and often found themselves in parts they were ill-equipped to play. The *nouveau roman* was also anti-transcendental and refused, said Robbe-Grillet, to be 'a prelude to the *beyond* of metaphysics', so transforming fiction and leaving it in the postmodern condition in which we still often find it standing bemused today.

The *nouveau roman* was soon to find its counterpart in cinema, in the *nouvelle vague* of Godard, Truffaut and Chabrol, which proved that the death of the Author leads to the rise of the *auteur*, showing that even in an ungoverned universe there is usually someone somewhere in charge. By having the scenery fall down a great deal and keeping other cameras in shot they proved that films were fictions simply about themselves, and indeed this was a time when all art became about itself, books being about the writing of books and buildings being about the building of buildings. Thus architecture became postmodern too and form stopped being a slave to function, which is why skyscrapers now have cabriole tops. All art became a fund of eclectic quotations from all other art and it was clear, as André Malraux said, that we now lived in the age of the imaginary museum, when all styles were simultaneously available. The imaginary museum was duly built, in the form of the Pompidou Centre, or Beaubourg, which does for a major public building what God might have done for humanity had he chosen to put the intestines on the outside of our bodies, rather than the other way around. Clearly a radical new style existed, expressing *our* temper, *our* spirit, *our* world, and *our* endless desire to quote bits of things we sort of thought we remembered but could not be bothered to go and check out properly. All that was needed was for this new spirit of 'reflexive-ness' to be given its philosophical underpinnings. Naturally it soon was and – possibly at the very moment when Mensonge was beginning to grow Parisian – the basic mood of Structuralism was being born.

Structuralism succeeded Existentialism, but did not entirely dispense with its atmosphere – probably one reason why, as John

Sturrock has pointed out, one still cannot go out and find a good Structuralist nightclub, though there is of course no shortage at all of mint-based, kiwi-fruited Structuralist cuisine (or at least there is a shortage, but it is there on the plate and you have to pay for it). It did however dismantle many of its premises, and convert the basements of some others. Sartre had claimed existence preceded essence, but the Structuralists showed this was not true, since in the world as they saw it there was neither. Where Sartre had held that man is a project who possesses a subjective life, 'as opposed to a fungus or a cauliflower', the Structuralists could not see any difference. Thus they disputed all the Being Sartre had been trying to recover from Nothingness and declared that Nothingness had won. Arguing that there is no ontological 'subject' in the sense of a continuous consciousness that knows where it is in the world, they proved it by stopping travellers getting off transatlantic jets and asking them what country they thought they were in. Thus Sartre's claim of choice – 'Man is what he makes of himself' – was illusory; when we stand before two doors, one marked by a figure in trousers and one in skirts, we have the illusion of choice but not the reality of it, since we are simply responding to signs, though the situation is different in Turkey. Above all, they disputed the entire tradition of the Cartesian *cogito*, showing that Descartes had quite misunderstood Montaigne, who had not been proposing the mind–body dichotomy at all but merely asking for the return of a book.

In short the Structuralists showed that our decisions have been constructed by language long before we even arrive, and the human condition does not resemble a man condemned to death for nothing but rather Terminal Four of Heathrow Airport. Philosophy was not concerned with Being or Nothingness, Plight or Alienation; it was a study of language. Saussure and his floating signifier was recalled into service, and for critics with the radical rigour of a Roland Barthes it now seemed that just sitting down of a night with Racine's *Phèdre* and working over the nature imagery was work more for a boy than a man. The time had come to take literary criticism out into real life, or far better real life in into criticism. Thus, developing what came to be called the *nouvelle critique*, Barthes displayed that critical method could be applied to almost anything, from all-in wrestling to advertisements for detergents – for, if everything is a form of language, everything can be read as if it were a text. We can imagine the powerful impact he must have had on the student Mensonge as Barthes sat down with his class in the café of an evening and read a plate of steak and chips with them, until at last they were told either to eat up or leave the premises. Here, then, was the philosophical world in which the Mensongian achievement was to be forged.

Of course steak-and-chips with Barthes was but one of many new intellectual experiences that made up the ambiance of Mensonge's novel thinking. By this date, the great Claude Lévi-Strauss had set aside his earlier work in the nether garment trade – rumour has it he had worked here with another French philosopher, J.-F. Lyotard – and was now producing a parallel revolution in the sphere of anthropology. Working with primitive Brazilian tribes, mostly in Paris, he was able to show that all societies are structured according to coherent myths which can be read as a system if one just remembers to displace all the signifiers into signifieds. Hence exactly the same codes or principles apply, whatever we happen to be doing within the culture – hunting animals, cooking food, building houses, inventing myths of gods, or exchanging wives – though he did acknowledge that some of these activities were quite a lot more fun than others. He also established that in most cultures women function as a basic unit of currency, or a rate of exchange, though not all hotel receptionists will accept them, which is why it is best to travel with a well-known credit card as well. He also demonstrated that the *pensée sauvage* was in no way different from the mentality of more cultivated societies. Thus, working, if from a fairly safe distance, with the cannibal Pukipuki tribe of Melanesia, he discovered that the explanation the tribe gave for eating only its most attractive young women was exactly the same as that given by L'Escoffier for rejecting thin and scrawny chickens and stewing only the fattest and finest, the only difference being that they charged less for the cover.

And, Mensonge would have realized, a similar great *boule-*

*versement* was happening in the field of history, where Michel Foucault was already making his powerful mark. Foucault was proving that all history happened at the same time and not in succession, as had previously been mistakenly thought. This realization stripped historical thought of its transcendental narcissism, as well as its myth of lost origins, and much else besides. Foucault revealed that there are no causes and no effects, or at least not in that order, and hence it was no longer possible to sit exam papers in the subject. Foucault was following the Nietzsche of *Ecce Homo*, where he showed the folly of all knowledge. He was able to prove the point by amassing a great deal of it and then not being able to show it had meaning, since any discourse could only be about discourse and not about any other thing. He had already shown that 'madness' and 'sanity', 'sickness' and 'health', were simply linguistic inventions derived from the prevailing systems of power and happened to be applied to people who were not too well mentally or physically. And Mensonge may well have known that Foucault was already beginning to conceive, if that is the word, his monumental six-volume *History of Sexuality*, and declaring that sexuality was 'a field of signs calling for decipherment', a message very close to Mensonge's own work. To this day we are not at all clear who excited whom first – was it Foucault Mensonge, or Mensonge Foucault? What we do know, however, is that in the matter of publication at least, Mensonge was to come, as it were, first.

One other possible early influence should also be mentioned. This is the Parisian psycho-analyst Jacques Lacan, a man whose command of Freud's corpus has been widely recognized as unique. Indeed his adaptation and conversion of Freud's thought to the atmosphere of Paris in the 1950s is one of the great triumphs of intellectual conversion, comparable to the coming of the McDonald's Hamburger just a few years later. Aware that the French found it difficult to accept the entire notion of the Unconscious, since, in the great spirit of *clarté*, they assumed that the Unconscious was simply confirming what they had decided in all logic to do, Lacan was able to show that the Unconscious was really another writing system, 'structured like a language', and that fortunately the language was French, and not German, and was therefore much wittier than had been supposed. Showing that what we call dreams are actually a series of bedtime puns on French words, he was thus not only able to still French suspicions, but actually to establish the domination of French culture *even at the level of the id*. It is certainly not hard to see the relevance of all this to *La Fornication comme acte culturel*.

So the Paris in which Mensonge, whatever his habits, must surely by now have arrived was a place of extraordinary new ideas, ideas that would dominate the thought of the next twenty years. The displacement of the subject and its replacement by language; the awareness that culture was a system of signs traded at different rates of exchange; the elimination of all metaphysics and transcendental presences; the demythologization of bourgeois identity, the desacralization of the structures of power, and the deconstruction of sexuality – all this was going on in the streets and cafés, and pouring into the alert mind of the philosophical young Mensonge. As he went about his fire-eating or wrote his reviews of the plays he so steadfastly refused to see, Mensonge must have been brooding, teasing, questioning, doubting, discovering, and trying to relate what were still many disparate strands, pointing this way and that. What everyone was waiting for, everyone needed, was the coming of the centreless centre, the presentless present, the writerless writing, the signless sign that would draw everything together and put it into its true lack of relation. Evidently what was called for was a great coming together, an ultimate *jouissance*. But who would provide it? Encyclopedic as they were, none of the major thinkers seemed yet to have produced the summative deconstruction, the supreme negation. Happily, as we now know, or think we do, there was one. The book that would put the pieces together by pulling them apart was, in some quiet room, already being written. And its author, or rather not its author, but the reader who first wrote it, was none other, or probably none other, than Henri Mensonge.

# 7

Just what Henri Mensonge did to change the face of modern philosophy we will come to in a moment. But at this point in the narrative it is probably as well if I try to explain how I – or the ego that chooses to bear my name – should first have become so interested in the philosophy, and engaged in the strange and obscure history, of this important man. I am, I suppose I should tell you, a gentle and scholarly sort of person, accustomed to rising quite late in the morning, after my wife has gone out to paid work, and submitting myself to the rigorous disciplines and duties of the study: sharpening pencils, making myself cups of coffee, moving papers about, typing a letter to the attractive girl in the post office with whom I seem to have struck up something of a friendship, and in this way and that gradually immersing myself in that demanding welter of scholarly activity and ratiocination that has so long, and so satisfyingly, filled my life. I am, I have always supposed, simply an old-fashioned scholar, not usually drawn to the latest trend or the newest fad. Indeed my real work lies in the planning, and perhaps one day even in the producing, of a new edition of the work of the Elizabethan poet Chidiock Tichborne (1558?–1586), so sadly omitted from the new *Oxford Companion to English Literature*, whose very brief *œuvre* has long required serious rehabilitation. I became in due course attracted to the work of three very fine scholars – the Argentinian Chestertonian and gnostic, J. L. Borges, the Russo-American Pushkin scholar and lepidopterist V. V. Nabokov, and the Franco-Irish Cartesian S. Beckett – and, discovering that all three wrote fiction in their spare time,

I gradually acquired a modest scholarly interest in the matter.

Probing further, I was soon to learn that their delightful if occasional fictional musings had somehow succeeded in exciting the admiration and imitation of a whole body of young American neophytes, who had determined to take the modern novel further down the path of experimental obscurantism from which, during the 1950s, it showed dangerous signs of diverting. These young men – Barth and Barthelme, Coover and Carver, Gaddis and Gass, Sorrentino and Sukenick, to name but eight, or possibly four – were writing a contemporary American fiction that shared a good deal in common with the *nouveau roman*. So they courageously chose to dispense with plot, character, beginnings, endings, and no doubt in some cases publication itself. This, I learned, was the new art of Postmodernism, and naturally I became an *aficionado*. I discovered how to derange my senses a little, found out how to tell a Hawkes from a Handke, rearranged my library in anti-alphabetical order, in the postmodern way, learned to conduct myself sceptically before reality, and soon found myself something of an expert on sur- and meta-, super- and post-fiction. Before long I was much in demand for small lectures in obscure halls to thoughtful and promising groups among whom these matters naturally stimulate the most intense excitement. Seeking an explanation for the underlying philosophy of this fiction of disordered codes and lexical playfields, I found myself reading in the background criticism. This led me to the Structuralist and Deconstructionist revolution, which was, I realized, doing no less for the future of philosophy than the post-novel novel was doing for the future of fiction.

Of course I was hooked, and I began reading intensively in the matter. It was not long before it was dominating my thinking and my writing – or, as I came to understand, the other way round. So, over the last ten years or so, I have found myself spending most of my waking hours, which in any case are not very many, pursuing the more recondite paths of the subject, chasing the odd floating signifier here, reading the obituaries in the London *Times* to keep up with the Death of the Author there, and so on. Today I think I can claim to have made a fair mark in the field. Thus, in the matter of the 'learned sock' of Walter Benjamin, which has occasioned much dispute about whether a sock is full or empty, I was able to show in a scholarly way that Benjamin had small knowledge of socks at all, preferring to stuff his shoes with old manuscripts by Kafka whenever the weather was inclement. Similarly decisive was my intervention in the great debate between Jacques Lacan and Jacques Derrida on the subject of Edgar Allan Poe's story *The Purloined Letter*, a famous Deconstructionist crux. I was fortunate in being able to demonstrate that the letter was in fact not purloined at all, but simply lost down the back of a settee and recovered by Poe at a later date. I have produced a reasonably momentous work on hegemonic paradigms in a suburb of North Leicester, relating late Althusserian concepts with those of the middle Laurie Taylor. And I have also published, in the magazine *Pos*, several important pieces in the radical misreading of literary texts, mostly without quite intending to.

Thus my services are frequently sought, though, as a good Borgesian, I rarely leave my desk and bother to venture out into the world, it having been proved an inadequate concept anyway. Certainly I am not one of those new Turbo-Profs, or Club Class modern scholars, who are constantly jetting around the world with their Vidal Sassoon haircuts and their code-locked executive briefcases, lecturing here for the British Council in Belgrade and there for the Goethe Institute in Copenhagen, now for the Rotary Club in Toronto and then for the hundred-dollar-a-plate literary brunch of the Save-the-Whale Club in Dallas, Texas, like so many of my academic colleagues these days. Nor am I any sort of devotee of that grotesque modern invention, the academic conference, having never been one for plastic name-tags, paper hats, wolf-whistles and conga lines through the dining room, not even in the privacy of my own home.

However, a few years ago I was invited on the strength of my work to take part in a 'world literary congress', one of those events of which I have been told much but of which I have had little real experience, sex being another. These absurd occasions are usually held, my academic colleagues have warned me, in some distant sultry clime where the endless sun gives you a headache, the repeated slap of the surf on the shore maddeningly intrudes on some serious debate on optative counterfactuals in elegiac works, and the troublesome clatter of ice in cold drinks ruins evenings when your only wish is to get fully up-to-date with the work of your peers, many of whom you have not set eyes on since you left them after lunch at the Gay Hussar restaurant in Soho at least two days before. So stern had been my friends' warnings about the unpleasantness of airport VIP lounges, the difficulties of carrying duty-free whisky and tobacco over long distances, the irritating manners of airline stewardesses, persistently soliciting you to take chickens kiev and brandies of which you have no need, and the plagues of endless room-service, excessive towels and pornographic cable television which now besmirch so many foreign hotels, that I have always made a point of rejecting such invitations at once, preferring to stay at home to make sure that the roof stays on and the dustbin is properly emptied.

Thus, when a few years ago I was solicited by telephone to attend some International Literary Festival of this type, I was at first quite sharp with my refusal, having been given some very dismaying accounts of occasions of just this sort. Normally, I understand, there is a very old Nobel prizewinner from somewhere like Chad who has long since ceased to write but wishes to make a very important statement about the development of the ode in the Third World. There is a large delegation from Russia there, to remind writers of the importance of writing about brotherhood, amity and concord, with special reference to the next grain harvest, and an even larger delegation from the United States, there to remind writers not to, and wishing instead to talk about the Great Advance in American fiction, which then turns out to be a cash one. The French come and insist that everything be translated by interpreters into their own language, even the menus in French restaurants, and the British come and ask for it to be translated back again. The entire proceedings must be listened to through headsets, which apart from spreading infection also normally prove faulty, so that one ends up listening to the comedy channel, hosted by Alan Coren. Important resolutions are always passed, against fate, and death, and in favour of eternity, and also about the need for more women at the next congress in five years' time, when those male writers who are not already past it will be. Then addresses are exchanged, love-contracts are sealed forever, and it is back to reality, which theoretically does not exist, and to the wife, who may, along with the bag of dirty laundry, which most certainly does. It will not surprise you to learn that I declined.

However, my caller, a young lady clearly professionally trained in the arts of telephonic seduction, was insistent. She made it clear that, should I fail to attend, the advance of scholarship would grind screamingly to a halt. Moreover I would embarrass an audience of thousands, mostly Heads of State and Ambassadors, who would cross wild terrain in order to hear me. Doris Lessing and William Golding, Margaret Drabble and John Fowles, Christine Brooke-Rose and Barbara Taylor Bradford had already said yes – but only on condition I attended. Somehow assent was pressed from me, and hence a few weeks later I found myself packing my diarrhoea tablets, and filling large wallets with many kinds of money, on my way to this occasion.

I had understood from the imperfect telephone call that our venue was in Austria; instead I found myself headed for some antipodean location or other. This involved a flight of several days in the steerage of a fully-packed jumbo jet on which, for some reason, every passenger had been assigned to seat number 55F, where I happened to be sitting. The quarrel that this occasioned had still not been resolved by the time we landed at our first stopover, Pellagra, having by then overflown innumerable cultures and ways of life, thousands of years of history, and uncountable living individuals while staring at four mediocre films with faulty sound-tracks, all starring Chevvy Chase. Signs of cholera and general panic were already breaking out by the time we reached our destination 'down under', where they sprayed us with flit guns before allowing us into the country. A small delegation of cultural persons met us at the airport and gave us each a stuffed koala bear before, as they put it, onwarding us to the northern state where the congress was, under extreme equatorial conditions, to be held.

On arrival all one's worst expectations were promptly fulfilled. Lessing and Golding, Drabble and Fowles, Brooke-Taylor and

Bradford Rose were absent, or not present, having sent transparent excuses. The reception was held at the local broadcasting station, so that world-famous writers could be televised live falling over as the local four-X ale hit them. Four more beer receptions followed before we were carried to the buses and driven deep into the local rain-forest, where, we were told, the intellectual part of the proceedings would take place. Somewhere deep in the bush a beneficent nature and a cunning state governor had conceived a site for a modern academic campus so remote that no living centre of population could ever be corrupted by it. Kookaburras screeched from the gum trees, our hosts appeared to be naked apart from a tattered denim garment worn about the thighs, and we were bedded down in student dormitories with three other conferees, two of whom spoke a Finno-Ugrian dialect and the third no known language whatsoever.

I was prepared to do less than enjoy the congress which followed, but in the event – and I am told that this frequently happens with congresses – my worst expectations were confounded. The writers, though ill-read, proved affable, and showed the dog-like devotion towards the scholar and critic that one naturally expects but all too rarely receives. The campus proved a treasure-trove of contemporary thought, being staffed largely by *émigrés* from Islington who had fled the neighbourhood after the disappointments of 1968 and were now teaching Althusser and Kristeva to the local students. Most of these, as it happened, came straight off the sheep-stations, and clearly knew no other clothing than shorts and thongs. Yet, despite the fact that their normal mode of address, when seeing one another in the corridor, was a hearty 'Up your bum, mate', they had evidently proved more than fertile soil for the courses on the difference between early and late Foucault that made up the bulk of the curriculum.

It was hardly surprising that Structuralist and Deconstructionist approaches should play a large part in the proceedings, rather to the amazement of the Mills and Boon contingent from London, and that my own lecture on 'Derrida or Deleuze, Two Views of the Hymen', should go down rather well. Our lectures were held out of doors, in the beating sun. This and the persistent tinnies that circulated through the company may explain why, when on the third day a speaker rose and began to speak of Henri Mensonge, our reactions were slow. It was towards sundown, if not duskup, and visibility was poor; there was subsequently to be much dispute about whether the figure who now set about engrossing us was actually Mensonge himself. The fact that he disappeared both subsequently and indeed previously made this seem probable; on the other hand, there was much talk of a famed Australian scholar living in the bush and writing a novel for the Booker prize who had been working on Mensonge's hermeneutic for many years. The lecture was an overwhelming experience, the wonder of a lifetime; and naturally I then set to work to make further inquiries about this to me new, and utterly radical, thinker.

Oddly, for it rarely does, fortune was to smile on me. A member of the local faculty, overhearing my questions, took me for a drink at some local billabong. There he revealed himself somewhat knowledgeable on the matter, having, he said, beanoed a winter away in Paris, and he was able to answer some of my less searching questions. More to the point, at some late instant in the evening, or probably the early morning, he reached into a capacious Australian pocket and withdrew a small and tattered book. This was my first sight of *La Fornication comme acte culturel*, and initially it was not promising. The copy was stained with various juices and seemed to be beyond repair. Nonetheless, after I had turned only a few pages, I found myself reaching into my own pocket and pouring out the contents of my wallet in a financial exchange. The young scholar was loath at first to part with his prize, but I promised him a good reference for a job elsewhere and a photocopy of my lecture. These promises, the financial goodies I was showering on him, and his general physical condition led him in due course to give way.

When I inspected the book more closely, I discovered that several pages were missing, and that my young friend had kept some coded account of his sexual conquests inside the front flyleaf. Even so I realized that I had come into possession of a rare and unusual treasure, that I had in my hands – or in one of them, for it is not a large book – a work that was likely to upset all my thinking and change my life, if not vice versa. I read and re-read it all the next day, missing speeches by two Nobel Prize winners and the Gallipoli Day sausage bar-b-q and seafood fryup. At first I was half resistant to its radical message, not being then inclined as I am now to grant the decisive intervention it was making. The speaker who was or spoke for Mensonge never returned, and several bottles of whisky went missing too. But there in that improbable down-under location, beneath the kookaburras and the gum trees, I found myself directly confronted with the overwhelming genius of Henri Mensonge.

I shall never forget that moment, that place, nor the difficulty we had, thanks to erroneous dates and airlines on the tickets, in returning home to anything resembling Europe. But during that endless flight on Bikini Atoll State Airlines, and the several fruitless weeks we spent in Guam while the plane was repaired, I simply could not wait to pursue and to declare my interest in Mensonge. In the many years since, I have devoted myself assiduously to the labyrinthine quest that started on that dusky evening 'down under'. I unearthed as much as I could of the work of the master, and am now completing a *bibliographie raisonnée* listing the works that could well be by him as well as the works that could well not be; as might be imagined, this should run to many volumes.

Though normally unwilling to leave my desk, I have taken numerous weekends in Paris, encouraged in part by the fact that the girl in the post office has quite a taste for it too. Here we have spent countless happy hours in the Bibliothèque Nationale and wandering the various *boîtes*, collecting reminiscences and half-hidden glimpses of the man who has done so much for the thought of our day. Above all, I have been attempting to collate an authoritative edition of *La Fornication* – no mean task, it must be said, since every copy seems somewhat different from every other, suggesting a life-style within the Imprimerie Kouskous rare in the history of printing. My aim has been simple – to introduce *La Fornication* to the widest possible public. This is what I trust I am doing now, though, of course, just how wide you will all prove to be is something we have yet to find out.

Nonetheless, of one thing we can be sure. One day Mensonge will finally be recognized, his place understood, his meaning seen. It will then be apparent that no one could have missed him, that he must always have been there. If I will thus have played some small part in lifting him from nowhere, and putting him somewhere, then I fancy my life, or one very small part of it, will not have been totally – despite what everyone says – in vain.

# 8

That is the story – all too briefly told, I fear – of how I first embarked on the now longstanding quest for the mystery and the meaning, the trace and the glimpse, of the prodigious Henri Mensonge. But, you will ask, just *what* was it, in the pages of that dirty little book I chanced to lay hands on in the antipodean jungle, that convinced me that I was in the presence, which would prove to be the absence, of one of the greatest, if not *the* greatest, of late twentieth-century thinkers? What can I say? Only that extraordinary intuition combined in that moment with my characteristic good judgement to show me I was in contact, of sorts, with the one man who had distilled our contemporary thought and thoughtlessness in the one way it *could* be distilled, proved beyond doubt that thinking could no longer go on in the undirected way it had for centuries but would have to be started all over again, had taken up in *La Fornication* a radically new and previously unachieved position, yet one that we should all shortly have to try to follow.

Of course, like all discoverers, I was foolish enough to suppose I was totally alone in my discovery, solitary in my high opinion. Indeed everywhere I looked on my return I found widespread evidence of the international neglect of the great Mensonge. I was alone, but not *entirely* alone. For as time passed I found to my surprise that there were in the world more like me. In fact it duly transpired that there was a world network of devoted Mensongians, admittedly most of them in the strangest places, who likewise acknowledged our man as their philosophic master (*maître philosophique*). They corresponded with each other, and indeed published, if on a very occasional basis, a *Mensonge Newsletter* which not only keeps us all well informed about the lack of knowledge we have of him, but runs quite a good wine club as well.

Nor was that all. As, in my Parisian researches, I reached back to that extraordinary, historical moment when Mensonge's tract made its sly, sleazy appearance in the lesser bookstores of Paris, on that crucial day in 1965, or just possibly 1966, I found it had not gone unnoticed. In fact many fine minds had already noticed what we now consider obvious, that this book was the harbinger of a new age, the hub of a great change, the text of the future, and for that matter a bargain at the price, though they had said nothing at the time. Talking to me now, they were all too glad to boast of it; and I should here acknowledge all the assistance I have had, not least from the Groupe René Tadlov at Paris III, undoubtedly the leading group in Postmodern studies in France, and devout disciples of Mensonge.

What they say is what is now self-evident: Mensonge's book was when the past stopped and the present started. It said that Existentialism was *finito*, that Structuralism was *kaput*. It announced a new spirit yet to come, the spirit we now call Deconstruction, and said that it was also over. It was in short the opening stage of a whole new way of thinking *the entire sum of which he had already predicted, and the logical conclusion of which he had already reached.* With Mensonge, it was clear, there was simply no way of going any further forward, and certainly absolutely none of turning round and going back. Twenty years on and there was no one in Paris who considered him or herself fully informed – and that meant everybody – who was not acknowledging that Mensonge's philosophy was the *dernier cri*, the ultimate version. In fact to that view there has been only one major and convincing challenge. It is ironic, perhaps, that this challenge should have come from none other than Mensonge himself.

Who knows whether it is his characteristic modesty, his rigorous intellectual honesty, or just the desire to be left alone that has made Mensonge declare publicly – or as publicly as he is able without being there – that the book is of no importance, has no significant meaning, was just a joke to quiet a tempestuous mistress, and in any case is not by him? We cannot answer this definitively, but my guess is that it is a little bit of all of them, and also an expression of the Deconstructionist spirit at its witty best. For it is typical of Mensonge that when confronted with a book signed with his name he should not only deny authorship but try to implicate everyone else possible, from a certain Marie Carrotteuse to of course the forces of history, culture and language. 'Alas,' as he says (my translation), 'it was just a case of being in the wrong place at the wrong time.' 'So much the worse!' he said on another occasion over lunch with a friend we cannot now trace. 'Even if I had not written it – and which of us can possibly say whether I did or not? – *something* would have written *something* which would have been very much like it, though perhaps not with such good jokes.' 'The day had come, the time was ripe, the thought was waiting in the wings,' he is said to have told someone else we cannot find either. 'It was the best of times, it was the worst of times, it was the last of times, it was the first of times; and a far better man than I could have made a far better *Mensonge* of it.' Of course it all sounds like typically witty self-denigration – striking, perhaps, in that for once Mensonge is said to have uttered his own name in connection with his book – but I think we should see it for what it is, a supreme gesture of Deconstruction, as Mensonge seeks, by undermining it, to clarify the ultimate meaning of his work.

Indeed it was precisely this Deconstructive side that at first discouraged his contemporaries from taking Mensonge entirely seriously, and he was mistaken for an early Surrealist, or worse. This, of course, was absurd. From the start Mensonge was clearly a Post-Structuralist, acknowledging some aspects of the movement while firmly rubbishing others. Like Barthes, he acknowledged that philosophy was a science of signs, though not such big ones, and he agreed that everything could be read as a text. Like Foucault, he acknowledged the fundamental gap between words and things, but could not understand why everyone kept trying to close it. Like Derrida, he considered philosophy as a theory of non-perception or non-theory of perception, but did not think it made any *differance*. Like Kristeva (who feels sure she met Mensonge at a bicycle race in Lyons once, and shared some thoughts with him, and a packet of biscuits) he agreed that there is no privileged philosophical vantage point from which to see anything, or any thing, though unlike her he totally rejects the ability of consciousness to examine itself in any way whatsoever, or even remember what it did yesterday. In all this there are echoes of contemporaries and hints of successors. Structuralism, he agreed, had been going down the right path, but had nowhere near reached its logical conclusion. Now, he said, was the time to conclude it. The problem was that Structuralism had rightly pointed to the basis of philosophical crisis, which indeed lay in 'language', the logocentric tradition of Western thought. The problem was that having identified the crisis in language, the gap of the signifier and the signified, it then *continued to employ it*.

Thus it continued to sustain the illusory notion that it was possible for philosophy to *mean something*, so compounding the error in Western thought that had bedevilled it certainly since Plato, or maybe he said Kant. At the same time it had dispensed with a reality prior to language, so creating a situation where, as Mensonge put it, 'there is no about about for any thinking to be about, or for that matter not about'. What Mensonge was proving was nothing less than that *we cannot at once work in language and dismantle it conceptually*. In short, what Mensonge was proposing was not simply the relative but the *total* separation of the signifier from the signified, going on from Saussure but leaving him breathtakingly behind. This meant, as he said, either 'that we have everything to say, and nothing to say it with, or alternatively the opposite. Most of my philosophical contemporaries choose the one or the other, but quite frankly this looks like trouble to me.'

Here is our difficulty, our blockage, our impasse; here Mensonge opens up the essential double-bind of Deconstruction, now known as 'the Mensongian cul-de-sac'. Yet, if Mensonge's proposal that, in effect, we are written by a language we have no way of using left us very little, if not nothing, then Mensonge himself was perfectly prepared to face the fact. A series of gnomic propositions in various fleeting publications

63

clarifies, or perhaps obscures, the position he had chosen to take. 'All writing has always constituted an abuse. But today we must admit that it can only constitute itself as a self-abuse,' he said once in an illuminating review of a Peter Brook production which with characteristic rigour he refused to go and see. 'It is a condition of living now – or indeed at any other time, were we to prove capable of it – that we cannot hope to understand what we mean, any more than we can hope to mean what we understand,' he said on another occasion. 'What I say must be defined not by what it is, but by what it is *not*,' he said on a third occasion, or possibly later on in the second. 'And this applies to everyone else as well.'

Here, then, are the underlying Deconstructive premises – far more stringent than Derrida's – that reached their magical outcome in *La Fornication*. It is a tease of a book, at once at war with all the metaphysical certainties of the idealist tradition, while having no truck with the woolly humanistic equivocations of liberalism, the utopian idealism of Marxism, or the classic conservatism of the New Right. Acknowledging Nietzsche's view of the folly of all wisdom, it totally disagrees with him about the value of Wagner's *Ring*. Rebuking the *clarté* of the Cartesian tradition, it totally rejects the gnomic obscurity of the work of his philosophic contemporaries. Acknowledging Barthes's emphasis on the dominance of the text, it totally refutes his concept of *jouissance*, or textual pleasure-taking. 'Sex is difficult enough in bed, as my philosophic contemporaries should know,' Mensonge says sourly. 'To try to perform it in the bookcase is hubristic beyond belief. In any case it is no use pretending we are at a whorehouse when we know we are at a funeral. Try the book any way you like. It will show no sign of enjoying it, and will certainly not give a squeak back.' The same rigorous honesty is written into every page of *La Fornication*, a book that seems to resist any kind of interpretation. Indeed it positively *defies* the summary of the would-be interpreter, however intelligent and competent he may happen, as in this case, to be.

This poses considerable problems, since in order to establish the major importance of his book it seems necessary to establish what his book is about. Unfortunately, as Mensonge says, there is no about about for anything to be about, and that applies above all to his own work. Here we could say that it resembles any major work of art. 'A poem should not mean but be,' Archibald MacLeish once wisely observed in a poem. Unfortunately Mensonge, as is typical, takes this one step further, creating a book that does not simply refuse to mean but also refuses to be. In Deconstructionist fashion he insists that we cannot refer to any *purpose* in the text, any authorial *intention*, any historical *causes* behind the book, any *meaning* in its argument, any *effect* it might have on others or oneself. Today we have grown used to such difficulties with other Deconstructionist texts, but it must be said that the difficulties posed by others are trifling in comparison to the difficulties raised in Mensonge. Barthes, for instance, positively celebrates, teases and delights the reader with the text, asking us to enter its apertures and play with its dismemberments. Derrida invites us to supplement his deferrals in a state of endless foreplay. All this, however, is anathema to Mensonge, just another instance of 'la fornication comme acte culturel'.

In short Mensonge insists that we are all trapped within the walls of the Mensongian cul-de-sac – writer, interpreter, and, if you can get hold of the book, reader. As he says, here is the difference, or *différance*, between him and the others. What rigour requires, rigour must have. Walking down the path already dug by so many twentieth-century poets, he aims to write a book totally beyond interpretation, a book that not only resists but rejects us. He refuses to structure the work according to any laws of cause and effect, makes his style an anti-style, his mannerism a post-mannerism. Today it is all too clear that his choice of the lunatic printroom of the Imprimerie Kouskous was no aberration. His work is filled with all those gaps, ruptures, fractures, lacunae and apertures that have become a Deconstructionist mannerism, and then a few more. He deliberately clothes his style in the most complex of rhetorical devices – parataxis, metataxis, zeugma, synecdoche, catacresis and metempsychosis – though, confusing us further, not in that order. Of his determination to outwit us totally there can be no doubt. Unfortunately on the one hand, but perhaps fortunately on the other, he has not quite entirely succeeded. For his revolt against Cartesian *clarté* was modified by his even greater revolt

65

against a Derrida-ian obscurity, and the result is a book that, though very *scriptible*, is in passages quite remarkably *lisible* too.

Not that this totally solves the problem; Mensonge has left a few extra difficulties in the way, insisting for example that not only has he disappeared from the book as an author, but the words have disappeared from the book as a text, and in a sense it is *just not there at all*. 'This is not the book I did not write,' he has said, 'and I refuse to acknowledge it as not mine.' Yet another passage seems to say the opposite. 'My book must be read entire or not at all,' he comments in the introduction, which in French fashion characteristically comes at the end. 'Naturally I prefer the latter. You will find nothing in it, since that was all I could put there. Yet surely to read a book demonstrating the folly of thinking demonstrates the folly of thinking far less well than refusing to read it in the first place.' The elusive gestures continue. As he says in another passage for the reader foolish enough to have read on: 'This work should be considered as having been "written" entirely in "quotes", or better in " 'quotes' ". None of it says, little of it does, and all of it denies, says that it does not say.'

Perhaps, then, we may give the book a modern *misreading*? At one point Mensonge encourages us to think so. 'I agree with those modern scholars who insist to us that no interpretation can be anything other than a misinterpretation,' he notes, though adding with typical irony, 'Of course, I may have misunderstood them.' Momentarily, then, we might take comfort from Paul de Man's idea of the *good* misreading ('By a good misreading, I mean a text that produces another text which can itself be shown to be an interesting misreading, a text which engenders additional texts'). Alas, Mensonge then goes on to deconstruct *that*, arguing that getting it wrong cannot logically be a version of getting it right. The fact is that Mensonge leaves the would-be interpreter nowhere to go except right up the Mensongian cul-de-sac where he himself appears to be, only for us to find he is not there. And here, surely, you see my dilemma. We are on a quest, you and I, for the meaning of Mensonge. To establish his importance we need to know the gist of his great book. Yet, as I have said, the likelihood of your obtaining a copy and making your own reading is small; the book is as scarce as virginity in California and a good deal more expensive. I suppose most scholars and critics would, to be honest, feel like throwing in the sponge at this point, and I am tempted myself. Certainly that would leave Mensonge, if he exists, in a state of high glee. But it is no way forward, if that is where we are going, and it leaves me with only one thing to do.

I have, in these circumstances, and in these circumstances alone, decided that after some sleepless and troubled nights to defy Mensonge *just as he defies us*, and attempt to offer in what follows a brief account, an imperfect summary, of the contents of his contentless work. It is and must be a misreading, a version of a version. I would like to think it a good misreading, a first-class misinterpretation – though Mensonge himself proves this impossible, and he is always right. I ought to explain my methods. I will attempt to quote, or 'quote', extensively, though this of course has its problems, not only because Mensonge says that the entire book is itself a quote from a quote, but because of variations between different states of the text – which shifts in length, I have discovered, from 39 to 115 pages depending on the copy, and constantly disputes with what may be previous or alternatively subsequent versions of itself. All translations must be my own, there being no other; however, because translation itself is, as Saussure has shown, impossible, a deviant misreading, I should prefer myself not to be quoted by anyone. I have tried to retain the spirit of Mensonge's eccentric and complex style, which has sometimes been compared with that of Jonathan Swift, though in fact his work lacks Swift's sunny benevolence and optimism. But there is a style of incongruous wit which some have regarded as the distinctive Mensongian signature, enabling us to identify when he is writing, even when he may not be. In some cases I have silently corrected obvious errors, though this could very well be an obvious error. I would like to believe that all this will convey to you some impression of the meaning and the message, the importance and the influence, of *La Fornication comme acte culturel*, though Mensonge says it has none of these whatsoever. You know, quite frankly, and just between ourselves, it is no easy business just trying to be an ordinary workmanlike scholar these days.

# 9

I now reach the truly difficult task of this book – the task I have been too long dreading and too long deferring, as if by trying to supplement or defer it it would never arise. Clearly there is no way to celebrate Mensonge's significance and magnitude *other* than by giving a summary of his great masterwork *La Fornication comme acte culturel*. That, apart from an old handkerchief or two, is all we have of him, perhaps all we will *ever* have of him. And yet, and yet . . . The difficulties seem intense, my timidity all too understandable. It is a task that can only be performed against the implied, no, indeed, the expressed wishes of Mensonge, or rather his text (let us, provisionally, call it 'his' 'text'). Those wishes may reveal his desire that the book be read only properly and in full; but full is not a Mensongian word, and they rather express his wish that it be kept unread and totally empty. Moreover, if, after many troubled, sleepless nights, one did summon up the – what shall we say: courage, gall, veniality, desire for recognition? – to go ahead despite his strict prohibitions, the most appalling problems still remain. For *La Fornication* can not only be called the greatest unread work of our times; it is explicitly designed to remain that way. The many major scholars I have consulted, often by long-distance telephone at my own expense, are adamant in saying that this is a work of such profound intellectual subtlety, linguistic density and textual disorder that there is no way even of translating it, never mind understanding it, and that only a person of the most limited imagination, and probably the most unmitigated stupidity as well, would even dream of undertaking the task. Fortunately for the common reader, there are just one or two of us who possess exactly those qualifications and are prepared to use them. Or maybe I am too modest. Just casting one quick eye round the world of journalism and scholarship, I realize there could well be hundreds.

So, perhaps. Toulouse-Lautrec once observed that it is when the great man refuses the task that the smaller one has his opportunity. I am perfectly prepared to accept, as I have had to, that I am just a minor worker in the field: one of those who in the great domed library of scholarship sits furthest from the issue desk at the end of the longest row and has to wait an eternity for the books he ordered to come, only to find them the wrong ones. I am a footnote to a footnote, a sub-sub-sub-librarian: call me Ishmael and I perk up immediately. I seem to have nothing to lose and everything to gain. My reputation certainly cannot grow any less, and just might grow a little more, from nothing to something. Another publication could be worth another salary increment. The opportunity has come, my moment is here, and with a new English-language translation of *La Fornication* just beginning to luff over the horizon it is not going to stay for much longer. And yet, and yet . . . Even now something – is it torpor, or worse? – urges me to delay, defer, put off, by any means, from cleaning the oven to giving a lecture in Rochdale. The pen when reached for does not seem to rise, as if it is telling me something about the unsatisfactory nature of the whole project. Yet, as both our new Deconstructionists and British Rail keep telling us, a delay, however good, does not last forever. Yet Mensonge himself would disagree. Indeed, if we could say that *La Fornication* had anything so vulgar as a gist, this would probably be it: that there is no point in aiming at the peak or coming to the crunch, for in logic there is no peak to peek at and no crunch to crunch on. And yet, and yet . . . No: I insist on commencing.

Let us first consider the title, which is said not to be Mensonge's title at all. There are cynical scholars who have suggested that it was carelessly borrowed from another book, or supplied by the publisher for gross and venial reasons. I believe them to be wrong, for though the title does not convey the book's real meaning (and gave the book a not entirely deserved sale among the 'I am over 21 and a serious lover of art' brigade), nor would any other title either. The fact is that, like so many great works of French philosophy, the book's ostensible subject is not its real one. Mensonge makes this perfectly clear, if I have understood him aright, which I probably have not. 'Only in the most incidental sense is this a book about sex,' his preface tells us. 'I am neither a lecher nor a Freudian, and only by adoption a Frenchman. In France, of course, there is nothing in the least new in proposing sex as a major matter of interest. My originality – it could well be my only one – is precisely that I do not.' And a later passage puts the matter with even greater explicitness: 'With fornication we may, I suppose, do one of two basic things. We may lie back and think of France, and probably nowadays all the rest of the Common Market. That is what most of my colleagues like to do. Alternatively, we may stand up and analyse it, thinking of logic, philosophy, thought itself. It will come as no surprise to any who know me, though none do, that I have chosen to do the latter, especially after my experiences with the former.'

The thrust, or lack of it, of Mensonge's intention should not therefore be misunderstood. What he is seeking to do is just what French philosophy has often thought it was doing, indeed hinting that it had done, yet was somehow, perhaps because of the influence of the Gallic love-tradition of Heloïse and Colette, Sade and Genet, avoiding doing. And that is, quite simply, analysing sex *semiotically*, as just one more signifying system among the others, like Barthes's steak-and-chips. 'Simply summarized,' Mensonge says, 'the aim of my work is to put coitalism back into culture exactly where it belongs – of a piece with the skyscraper and the food-mixer, the Yale lock and the moon landing, the multi-storey carpark and the shorter working week. I shall show it is merely an attempt at signification and not an inherent value. Far from wishing to impose content on it, I wish to deconstruct what content it has seemed to have to so many. And especially, of course, to those of Gallic disposition.' Thus *La Fornication* – to the disappointment, one might imagine, of many early readers – has nothing at all to do with pleasure or pornography, desire or delight, stimulation or seduction, gratification or gustation, licking or slavering. Indeed this, says Mensonge, 'is why my enterprise is one of "genuine" " 'originality' " '.

Certainly it is this that distinguishes it from almost everything else in contemporary French philosophy, from Bataille's *Erotisme*, Lévi-Strauss's *L'Homme nu*, Barths's *Le Plaisir du texte*, Baudrillard's *De la Séduction*, Lyotard's *Economie libidinale*, and so on and so on. As Mensonge says, it is not hard to see what keeps French thought selling busily in the market place these days. 'Is there a metaphor in the text of philosophy?' Jacques Derrida asks in all apparent innocence in his 'White Mythology'. 'In what form? To what extent?' To this Mensonge gives his answer. 'You know, Jacques, you know,' he says. 'And you know what a sexy metaphor it is.' 'What the text says, through the particularity of its name, is the ubiquity of pleasure, the atopia of bliss,' cries Roland Barthes in *The Pleasure of the Text*. 'Roland, Roland, please,' comments Mensonge. 'Tell me, have you ever really *tried* one?' The Mensongian tone is far different. 'I propose to look at sex merely as an *interface*,' Mensonge explains coolly, 'even though I know all too well that other organs are involved. I look at it as aperture and boundary, place of slippage and sloppage, metaphorical centre, place of exchange (*bureau de change*). My good friend Claude [presumably Lévi-Strauss] has shown us the exchange significance of the cooking pot in wild thinking (*pensée sauvage*). What he does with the wok I propose to do with the coital act – in all its embodiments. Or rather its *dis*embodiments, for that is exactly my point.'

It could of course be protested – and there is usually one person on the back row who tries it – that this does not distinguish his work from, say, Foucault's prodigiously planned six-volume *History of Sexuality*, or indeed from the speculations of the parachute-suited bevy of gender workers who descended on the sexual field in the 1970s and established the basis of Contemporary Castration Studies. This is to mistake the issue; Mensonge was not only way ahead of all of them but stepping in a totally different direction. The feminist claim that language was a tool of masculine power was, he said, so obvious as not to be worth intellectual attention. Or, as he put it, 'Zut alors, je m'en fou, oui?' More important matters were to hand, not the problem of demystifying gender but that of demystifying sex itself. 'My concern is with the fornicatory act itself, *coitus sui generis,*' he explains in the book, 'with coitus as it stands or lies there, a vacant sign waiting to be read, if people would simply stop for a moment, if they can, and try to read it. Who will? Well, now at last you have Mensonge.' And so we do, or at least so we think we do.

So, briefly, what Mensonge appears in the first instance to be telling us in *La Fornication* is that, in the great era of suspicion, when almost everything else has been demystified, decon-structed, demythologized and designified, sex has not, has been somehow 'left up there, secure on its pinnacle, just as if it were *the sum of itself*', and *this is significant*. In another passage he puts the point even more lucidly: 'In a time when nothing is sacred, and everything is discounted, we have somehow succeeded in preserving sex as the sacred heart (*sacré cœur*) of our existence – which can only mean as a false heart, a heartless heart at the heart of our universal heartlessness.' Though all other signs have been rendered empty, that of sex 'remains *full*, a sign of plenitude, of presence'. For this logical absurdity there must be an explanation. In a passage worth underlining by anyone who is not using the library copy he offers one: 'Is it not clear then that the act of fornication is being used to sustain the unwarranted delusion of the realized subject – even though all our theory on every other matter tells us that there is no subject for us to realize, that all such passports to essence are forged?'

How is it, then, that in matters of sex and sex alone what Mensonge calls 'the pathetic English-Whig view of history as progress and promise, of going somewhere and getting some-thing from it', the myth of 'coitus as replenishment', managed to survive in the thought of our time? Like Foucault, though rather more quickly, Mensonge traces this 'privileging of sex' back to bourgeois origins, when, for reasons of property, privacy and genealogy, the mercantile classes made sex private and scarce to drive up its price and increase its surplus value. Scarcity is secrecy, Mensonge points out, and secrecy is scarcity, and this was the machinery that invented that complex apparatus of 'dress and disguise, modesty and pudeur, distance and spacing' that raised the erotic stakes, role-typed male and female as other than each other, mystified them, and turned them into self-concealing signs, those 'exaggerated signs of *difference*, most of which could be removed by any competent medical worker in a matter of minutes', on which so much historical time was subsequently wasted at the expense of other things, like philosophical study. It brought that impatient wish to 'lay bare the other' across 'the spaces of desire' which could obsess culture at every level, and occupy an individual an entire lifetime, especially if they kept on taking the pills. Even into the twentieth century the process continued.

Like Lacan, though with rather more laughs, Mensonge looks to Freud, 'the patriarch of all our confusions', to explain this. As he observes, if Freud had not existed someone would have had to invent him ('Of course someone would have fantasized or dreamed him, but would their unconscious have been witty enough to think of the cigar?') to construct the twentieth century and its sexual preoccupations, or, as Mensonge puts it, to 'discover America, which Christopher Columbus, just looking at Indians, had totally missed'. Thus Freud is 'the Viennese bourgeois prophet who, far from crying in the wilderness, is laughing in all the most expensive consulting rooms in upper Manhattan'. It was Freud who gave sex its twentieth-century location, 'safely locked in that deepest and most impenetrable of all bank-vaults, the Unconscious, where its price rose yet again and where we could not get at it without him, for of course he kept the only key'. And it was from the value added in the Freudian hothouse that, Mensonge tells us, the modern privileging of sex arose: 'So there came the great modern cry – from the bed, the bath, the kitchen table, the backseat of automobiles, or wherever else we celebrate these fleshly ceremonials – that desire is a value and has an outcome, that we can therefore reach a "fulfilment". Ah, deceitful word, sad illusion. For a moment's thought, if we paused long enough to have time for it, would disclose that there is nothing whatsoever to fill, nothing to fill it with, and no fullness there to be filled, except what we ourselves put there or had put there, depending on your angle of vision (*point d'appui*).'

But Mensonge, of course, was really attacking his own contemporaries and their notion of desire as discovery. Like everyone else, he assaults the Existentialists, those who, 'hungry for being at any cost', celebrated sexual utopia, attached fornication to liberation, and encouraged the dream of a libido which, freed of repression, represented 'real desire'. So evolved the great 'Woodstock utopia' where all gratification, sexual, political, linguistic and philosophical, was considered possible. The 'fiction of desire's sacred essence' passed to the liberationist gurus of the 1960s, from the resuscitated Wilhelm Reich, sitting in his orgone box, and Norman O. Brown, squatting in his hot tub, to those other 'prophets of the pratfall of the polymorphous perverse', who turned 'the whole of California into a mind and body blowing madhouse', and even diverted the British away from a far more important 'relational gap', which of course is that of class.

The 'false sacred essence, the diachrony of coitus', thus passed on right into Structuralism and Deconstruction itself. Not surprisingly, Mensonge reserves his most violent attack for his own philosophical colleagues. Thus, long before Derrida was even to notice it, Mensonge was pointing the finger at the 'transcendental phallus' of Jacques Lacan. Derrida was to complain that Lacan tried to make the phallus both the signifier of all signifiers, and the signifier of all signifieds. Mensonge put the point more tersely, speaking of Lacan's 'great phallusy', and sourly remarking, 'It is surely always a mistake to ask the phallus to carry a weight it simply cannot bear.' Thus came the philosophical illusion that desire and seduction represented the decadent distances and unfilled spaces that would allow language to survive and thought to go on thinking, when, as Jean Baudrillard puts it in *De la Séduction*, 'la séduction veille à détruire l'ordre de Dieu'. Today, says Mensonge sourly, the very role of philosopher has passed from that of ratiocinative thinker to that of louche voyeur (*louche voyeur*), for whom a night with a text is better than a night on the town, thinking has replaced Aristotle and Plato as role-models with Sade and Genet, and 'the invitation of philosophy is to lick with Lacan, slaver with Barthes, guzzle with Kristeva, tease awhile with Derrida'.

Today, Mensonge suggests, what he calls the '*Playboy* school of philosophy' reigns supreme. Lacan's 'great phallusy' is no incidental matter, Barthes's desire for seduction ('The text you write must prove that *it desires me*') no casual one-night stand. Nor, in case this seems to support the feminist argument, is this solely a masculinist emphasis; Mensonge comments on the 'illusory safe vagina' at the centre of feminist philosophical thought. It is all part of the same hidden essentialism that belongs to an age that thought itself beyond essentialism, the transcendentalism of an anti-transcendental school of thought. *Mauvaise foi* is not done with. Even today, says Mensonge, we are still asked 'to go between the sheets and there inscribe the phallusy that it is possible to leave *culture for nature*, resacralize a *pure reality*. What in our jouissance (*jouissance*) we seek to express is still nothing less than this: "When I come, the world goes." That is, history goes, language goes, philosophy goes. Thus the sexual act and its spectacular outcome (*émission spectaculaire*) still remains privileged, permitting us to see ourselves coupling not with a corporeal partner or partners but with a universal self, a transcendentally orgasmic ego, and so recovering ourselves at a unique price (*prisunic*). The sign that is gone is still there, indeed it is literally *made flesh*. One moment's Deconstruction would unlock the whole pretence, showing us that this is just another egotistical illusion, inscribed where we usually inscribe illusions – on the blankness of the void.'

Nor has Mensonge done yet. In a brilliant passage that out-Freuds Freud, but is too long for even me to quote, he shows that the 'coital sign', the 'illusory model of the scarce and sacred pudenda' is set wandering freely, and is written metaphorically on every department of our cultural life. It is there in the 'hidden laws' we use to build our homes, organize our cities, control the space between public and private. So the butler at the door, the lodge at the gate, the public hall of the private house, the naves of our churches, the long streets leading to fountained parks, are the rhythms and rituals of all our initiations, and they are based 'on the false analogy of sexual secrecy'. These 'labyrinthine paths of access and diversion, opening and closure, public and private, provision and denial, *routes barrées* and *sens unique*, are always leading to some dark enigma', provocations to desire that hope to claim 'for every inlet a meaning, for every aperture a secret, for every container a content'. Thus we construct what he calls 'an illusory metaphysical vagina', by which we seek to give sense 'to the world's random sign, to fill full, fulfill'. What is more this is structured into language – 'we ask our sentences to copulate, our grammar to generate, our periods to punctuate' – and because it is in language *it must be in philosophy itself.*

And here we come towards, if we can still use the term, the culmination of Mensonge's argument. What he is showing us is how deeply 'the lie of the realized subject' is secreted in the very task that seeks to undermine it. He asks us why, and comes to a daring answer – because it *protects nothing less than philosophy itself from otherwise total demythologization.* If the *deus* we thought *absconditus* is still present in contemporary thought, he is there for one reason, and one reason only: to safeguard the *language of thinking,* and so protect *the* cogito *by which we still hope to analyse the world.* This is why Lacan's 'great phallusy' remains standing, this is why 'the myth of the sacred metaphysical vagina' survives. It protects what he calls 'the coital *cogito*', for without the metaphor we lose the mind, which would have no way to know itself. After all, thought 'penetrates' or 'probes'. It 'conceives' an idea. Once a 'concept' is 'engendered', it must be 'reproduced' and 'disseminated'. The intellectual task itself seeks to unmask, strip, 'lay bare the thing as it actually is'. 'Alas,' says Mensonge, 'the "thing" as it is in actuality is not, for there is no thing, and actually no actuality for it actually not to be not in.' Thus thinking strives to preserve the presence it has seemed to destroy: 'What we evict so bravely from the front entrance we admit secretly again at the back, deluding ourselves we have found some fundamental difference, when of course there is none.' The great triumph of Mensonge's book is here, and it is nothing less than the proof of the delusory notion of philosophy itself, and the deconstruction of its false endeavour to maintain what he called 'the non-existent ego of the scholar him/her non-self'.

Here is the brilliance of Mensonge's study, which truly follows the consequence of Deconstruction's own logic – which must evidently lead to the Deconstruction of Deconstruction itself. From the start the job was done, the central task performed. As Mensonge says, that always had to be 'nothing else than the demystification – I prefer to say the "desexing" – of that illusory safe vagina that still exists not only in culture but deep in the mentality (*mentalité*) of every intellectual. It is to this task I have dedicated my work.' That work's great message is now clear: not just that sex is the falsest of all the signifiers, but that in demystifying it we discover the falsehood residing in *all* forms of exchange. As Mensonge sums it up: 'When we seek to exchange so-called self with so-called self, we are in fact exchanging *nothing with nothing*. In sex and, as we now see, in *everything else*.' And it is here the path comes very near to its close, in a fundamental deconstruction of intellectuality itself which is Mensonge's great contribution to knowledge, or rather to the end of it. In a few more brilliant Deconstructions, Mensonge stitches the whole thing up – deconstructing the 'great phallusy' in ways that were to excite the wild admiration of the feminist critics of the 1970s, and disproving the 'metaphysical vagina' in ways that were to excite their abusive rage; eliminating the 'coital *cogito*', and so both the concept and the conceptualizing subject; undermining the entire long-term possibilities of intellectual life; adding seventeen footnotes to sources very few of which any of us have been able to trace; and then himself disappearing off into virtually total obscurity. It is the great intellectual triumph of the age.

The achievement is amazing for a man we know little about and have not since been able to find – though, it must be admitted, there are certain contemporary philosophers very grateful for Mensonge's absence, and who hope it will last for as long as possible. However, for the most honest of us, *La Fornication* must surely stand as *the* ultimate work of Deconstruction, taking the movement to its extremity. Eliminating intellectual presence entirely, Mensonge places himself at the very end of philosophy. We can hardly doubt his ultimate claim for his enterprise – that he, or it, 'opens a brand new door to an entirely novel area of Deconstructive inquiry, and what is more the final door, one not even worth going through, for on the other side *there is simply nothing there*. This is his final truth, or almost. 'My aim, by now, must be clear, to deconstruct any illusion of fullness which permits the coital *cogito* to exist,' he says in some late phrases. 'What clearly follows is that I must Deconstruct myself, or any illusion of a self, capable of thinking a thought, that you may happen to be left with. I – "I" – do this not to *defer* meaning, to seduce your interest, promise a supplement, as all too often do those philosophical colleagues of mine who still see long and well-paid careers stretching out in front of them. I wish to *withdraw* meaning, to *withdraw from* meaning, in a word to *subtract* or *decoitalize* myself, so avoiding any impression that you have been reading – impossible word – philosophy.'

So we come to the final stage of Mensonge's argument, which has particularly baffled many who have discussed it, especially late at night. This is the passage where, emphasizing that 'the lie of the realized subject is with us more often than we think, or "think" ', Mensonge, in one flamboyant last move, completes his crucial Deconstruction of himself and what he has done, breaking with his role as philosopher, with his book, his existence. This coda reminds us that the entire point to his argument is that we may find no entire point to his argument. Thus he and we, *langue* and *parole*, *signifier* and *signified*, arrive at the end of the Mensongian cul-de-sac (*impasse*) only to find that none of us are there. Certainly Mensonge is not. 'If you have read this far, you have read too far,' he says in some obscure final phrases. 'If you are here, you should not be. You have followed my seduction . . . but I did not mean to seduce. You have accepted my conception . . . but I have shown you I cannot conceive. You have followed me to my culmination . . . but I did not mean to culminate. One of us at least should not be here, and I think it is probably me.'

Yet even this formulation does not seem to suit him, and the book ends in a strange scatter of fleeting phrases. 'Here you have my summation, where I have come to,' he mutters at the very last. 'Do not allow it to satisfy you, for nothing satisfied me. If it does, I would have failed, as of course I have had to, or some "I" did who is not and cannot be "I", who must necessarily be nothing, is not capable of a thought, who cannot let even this be a thought, who cannot conceive, will not be conceived, who has desired what desire cannot give and desires only undesire, who is a supplement to what cannot be supplemented, a non-thinking non-subject who has   never been, who   cannot be, who   will not become, who   will not be coming, is not   even a name, not   even a word, not even the word   me   en   songe (requiring completion).'   And with that, somewhere in cryptic mid-sentence, Mensonge, or 'Mensonge', the one we have thought was Mensonge, if such a 'thought' is possible, absents himself, absents us, becomes not here, not there, in a way that anybody who takes philosophy at all seriously cannot possibly ignore.

# 10

So there we have it. I have tried, as best I can, but acknowledging in the Mensongian way the limits of human language, human thought and my own human nature, which I seem not to have any more, to present at least a glimpse or version of the achievement of what is surely our time's best philosopher, our time's finest work of thought. I have no doubt more time still will have to pass before the world at large comes to see it like that. But I trust it is now evident why many people, very thoughtful people, or so they were once, regard Mensonge's book as *the* ultimate work of Deconstruction, the 'fullest' and most 'complete'. Of course they undermine Mensonge's intention by doing so, but unlike him they have not yet found a way around that. It is clear that in one sense Mensonge's was the last book, the book that completes and concludes the shelf of modern thought. Mine must be by definition supererogatory, and I myself a small scholarly appendage to a major figure. But my book is here, and at a bargain price, and his is not; we need to know these things, even though knowing is impossible. I suppose it has all been worth it.

And Mensonge? In that one sudden and unexpected book, one brief moment of sudden luminosity, he 'came'. And in it, having come, he went again, and even after twenty years of meticulous dogsbodying we are still not sure whither. Since that time he has not, or not in a way we can regard as certain, chosen to write another *langue* or *parole*, and certainly no successor to *La Fornication* has shown sign or signifier of appearing. Twenty years, and that haunting silence continues! In one sense that was inevitable, given the basic message of his work – which is that there is not only no philosophical object of attention, but also no agent capable of doing the philosophizing. No agent, one says, and yet there does seem to be just the one. So, though we cannot but be forced to acknowledge the total rightness of his devastating conclusion, we must also regret the silence that it so inevitably led to. We can only hope that he will come to regret it himself, change his mind, rescind the absence, become the presence. He has every reason to do so, for the moment he shows up we will all be standing there ready to welcome and celebrate him.

But if Mensonge, the 'laureate of absence', as he has been dubbed, has gone from print and public, his trace most certainly has not. His claim that he has opened 'a new field of desacraliz ing inquiry' has proved more than justified. Indeed, there is very little that has been done in the last twenty crucial years in the fields of deconstruction, feminism, sociology, philosophy, social anthropology and all the other crucial subjects of our time which appears *not* to show a clear Mensongian imprint. There can be no doubt at all that philosophy has been quite different since Mensonge: more assertive and yet more elusive, more potential and yet more abstemious, more pressing yet more uncertain, more flirtatious yet less available, more present and yet more absent.

The Deconstructionist movement which Mensonge both started and finished has managed to continue after a fashion, an event after the event, but with a distinctive, odd air of finality – as if this all must be the last fling of the season, the final dismantling and pulling-to-pieces, the preparation for the winter that must come before we face the uncomfortable cruel spring of the coming new millennium. It has had its own severe mortalities, and many of those who were alive when Mensonge was are no longer with us, and probably in a far more complete way than Mensonge himself. They have left us with much unfinished business, but perhaps all along it was, as Mensonge suggests, simply *deferring* a finish that he saw from the start. Certainly we may think of all these airs of finality that are not finalities, these future promises that betoken no future, as bearing the ambiguous burden of the Mensongian vision.

As for Mensonge's elusive way of thinking, that remains with us. The difficult path he trod we still walk along. Questioning the entire competence of essentialism and metaphysics, he would of course have had no truck with the woolly equivocations of liberalism either. Challenging the traditionalism of the conservatives, he totally refuted the utopian idealism of the romantic left. Accepting some of the tenets of Marxism, like the need for faster trains, he utterly undermined the pseudo-scientific basis of their historical thought. Acknowledging Nietzsche's judgement on the folly of all wisdom, he was still unable to sit through an entire performance of Wagner's *Ring*-cycle. He shared the views of some of his own philosophical contemporaries, but always held them in a very different way. There were those who said his wavering path was leading nowhere; we now know he proved them decisively wrong.

So the work proceeds. Of course the 'fornicatory analogy' he demolished still lasts on, but has grown a good deal more elusive, perhaps as a result of herpes and AIDS, which has turned erotic attention off in quite new directions, towards such things as offshore banking and architecture. Indeed the general waning of sex we see all round us would not have surprised him one bit. As he said once: 'It is not my intention to eliminate fornication entirely, simply to make us look at it in a quite new way.' The transcendental phallus has certainly not been doing very well lately; the metaphysical vagina just may have been having a rather better time of it. The attempt of the new feminists to give ovarian writing a meaning that has gone from the phallic text is probably best understood however as a desperate attempt to elude the great Mensongian cul-de-sac, by claiming that they have something he has not, as well as not having something he has. But the fact that whole schools of criticism and philosophy are, having assimilated the Structuralist-Deconstructionist message, turning away from it altogether, and looking to new fields like landscape history for assistance, suggests how well the painful lessons of our absent thinker have been learned. No, the world is not at all the same as it would have been had Mensonge never existed at all.

*Never existed at all!* I wonder . . . The name of Mensonge, as I say, has left its clear and lasting imprint on the future of philosophy, such as it is. Some of his successors have gladly acknowledged his importance, while others have preferred to stay silent. Rumour has it that one of those who has been generous in his acknowledgement, albeit in private and unbuttoned moments, is Jacques Derrida himself, who has even admitted that, as far as he was concerned, Mensonge made quite a lot of *différance*. Curiously, only the other day I was looking at – these days 'reading' would be far too strong a word – a recent study by this admirable and subtle prophet, called *Signéponge/ Signsponge* (trans. Richard Rand, Columbia U.P., 1984, 160pp., $20, the proceedings of a seminar on 'The Thing' at Yale University). Some have found this work baffling beyond the usual, but I have to say I found myself very struck by his rather Lacanian argument, and thought I recognized just a faint sign or floating signifier of exactly the same instinct – should one describe it as thinking, or should one call it wit? – that has always seemed to me the hidden mark of Mensonge. In this book Derrida leads us into the strange 'abyss of the proper name', which, of course, the modern death of the subject and the modern language of signs threatens with dethronement. The subject – 'subject!' – of this book is the French poet and writer Francis Ponge, on whose name the title puns. Derrida in fact has been struck by the frequency with which sponges and sponge-like things occur in the writings signed 'Francis Ponge', and suggests that the poet in effect constructs his own name and own existence out of these lexical items. Ponge is said to have attended the seminar where Derrida read from his book, and largely agreed with him.

As I say, the mood seemed Mensongian, and my speculations were driven further. Derrida explains that *Signéponge* is about – 'about!' – 'the link (be it natural or contractual) between a given text, a given so-called author, and his name designated as proper'. And he asks us if Ponge 'had had another name, and if by some incredible hypothesis he could still have been the same person, would he have written *the same thing*?' Is it perhaps possible, by the same incredible hypothesis, that *Mensonge* had another name? If he had, would he have written *another thing*?

And is it – the thought grows more daring – possible that *Derrida* had another name? Could it be that the other name of each one of them was none other than the name of . . . ? Is it then just conceivable . . . ? 'Conceivable!' Of course, the word can no longer be said, or written. And these important speculations are really too difficult for someone like myself, an ordinary scholar. No, we should stick to the facts, such as they are, or in Mensonge's case, mostly are not. Nonetheless, the quest goes on, and I am prepared to guarantee now to all of you that I will not be turned away from it. Mensonge has to be made visible, and I have not only done but mean to keep on doing my best.

Yet, as I had to admit from the very beginning of this brief flight, Mensonge not only was in his prime but still remains the least known of the great Deconstructionists. I have indeed done my best to remedy that, but still, to be frank, have not got very far. His work, despite its reputation and its inordinate impact on the truly philosophically inclined, remains far too daring for general acknowledgement, though the first few budding foot-notes here and there suggest his spring is beginning. The *bibliographie raisonnée* goes on, and on, and on. And his life . . . ah well, his life. There are times, as I have complained already, when the biographical instinct despairs of itself. We keep finding this or that, but at the present low level of funding we are not getting very far. The people who think they can identify him, remember him warmly with gratitude, or assert they were his former mistresses generally turn out to be recalling someone quite different, in a hat. Facts that we thought we had secured frequently tend to disappear again. And since that one wonderful book appeared, Mensonge's intellectual heroism seems to have been absolute. Few of us have ever been absent with such total consistency. From time to time his appearance is reported, at some lecture or other, or performing some important academic duty, sometimes by doubtful witnesses but on other occasions by the highest and most reputable.*

* One report of great importance comes from Professor Frank Thistle-thwaite, formerly the Vice-Chancellor of my own University of East Anglia, and a source of the highest reliability. Knowing of my interest, he has kindly written to me as follows:

Now and again he is spotted, or said to be, at some major conference on an abstruse topic, such as the one I attended in the antipodes; but when these things are checked on not only does he not seem to have been there but the room he was booked

---

Dear Malcolm,

I greatly enjoyed your account of Henri Mensonge. I myself have a vivid memory of him. You may not recall (I think you were on study leave at the time, at All Souls or on one of those British Council Specialist Tours I know you like to take, researching some novel or other) that in the very early 1970s we invited him to the University of East Anglia when I was Vice-Chancellor to act as external assessor for the Chair of Medieval Cultural Linguistics. I fear we did not have an easy passage with him. He refused to reply to all correspondence, and Patricia Whitt's calls to Paris XX or wherever he was said to be then resulted only in much crackling and explanations that his whole department was 'fermé tous les jours'. However he clearly received the message because he duly arrived at the Maid's Head, called the university for chauffeuring, and was promptly whisked off for a Broadbent evening, no doubt intimate, as they always are.

The day of the interviews he was not at his best: bemused, I thought, and depressed by Norwich (he had hoped it was in America), the rate of exchange, and too much wine and cheese (his drink was whisky, preferably malt). However, the candidates for the chair – I think we managed to muster four – were clearly impressed by his presence, and the discussion rapidly became bi-lingual, or so it seemed to most of us. Certainly it did not make for clarity. There was a moment when two of your colleagues on the committee were clearly in some confusion: the lettrist thought Mensonge was discussing Lévi-Strauss and the historian Le Roy Ladurie. This did not help the candidates and in the upshot, as you will remember but too well, we were not able to make an appointment.

My last impression of Mensonge – if it was indeed he, for now you have made me doubt it – was of a dispirited leather jacketed *cher collègue* mounting an Eastern Counties bus for Cambridge, where he said he had friends in the English Faculty. It seemed an unlikely story at the time, and since living here in Cambridge we have not been able to confirm it. No letter acknowledging our hospitality ever arrived, though I doubt if he knew where he had been, and for some reason we never availed ourselves of his services again. But I am glad to see his work at last being given the homage due to it. Structuralism would certainly not have been the same without him.

Yours ever
Frank

into had disappeared as well. Rumours aplenty abound about his present whereabouts, and sightings are constantly reported in the *Mensonge Newsletter*, but these things yield few positive results. One has it that he has returned to Bulgaria, and that an article entitled 'T'ma, mgla, pizda', circulating recently under the cognomen G. I. Vranyovski in *émigré* circles in Munich, represents a total recantation of his position, and his conversion to Sufism. Yet another suggests that he is teaching in an obscure college in Wyoming under another name, probably Herbie. More extreme ideas are sometimes floated. There have been suggestions that he has on occasion thought of running for political office, and I suppose it is possible, but surely unlikely, that if he has indeed taken American citizenship he could eventually become the first totally absent president of the United States. Various books are sometimes attributed to him, but the idea that he could have written *Lace* seems to me a total canard. The most probable view, or the one I favour, is that he has simply retired quietly from sight and is living in impoverished circumstances somewhere in Provence, hunting for truffles, so far without any success.

As for recognition . . . Well, that continues to grow by the day, but very, very slowly. Mensonge has even been mentioned as a possible candidate for the Nobel Prize, but so protean are his talents that no category seems quite to fit him. My own university – rather pressed by me – recently awarded him an honorary degree, which was taken of course *in absentia*. It is known for something resembling a fact that Yale has tried hard to recruit him, and offer him its Dunlop Chair of French Letters, but that all correspondence has been returned marked *whereabouts not known* – oddly enough, the title of a very early essay we think to be by him. Commentary remains thin, perhaps mainly due to the shortage of other commentary to quote from. Of course there is the invaluable *Mensonge Newsletter*, which would be delighted to receive subscriptions, which I am very willing to forward. And there are the first signs of something like an account of his work in a few usually inadequate articles in the odd small French *journaux*, or else in the various English-language periodicals with names like *Prod* which spring up like mushrooms from the smaller American university campuses. In Paris the Groupe René Tadlov has done sterling work on him, and small cells of Mensongian scholars exist in Stuttgart and Cardiff. I myself take some pride in having first introduced him to the British public in a small article in the London *Observer*, which appeared on 1 April 1984. Yet of one thing we can be certain. If the twentieth century is ending, as it is, in a state of profound intellectual self-questioning, if not confusion, that is surely due to the hidden impact of Mensonge. His model of consciousness is undoubtedly the one we recognize as our own, his unique sense of vacancy is for us a true sign. *La Fornication comme acte culturel* is, unquestionably, one of the few books of our time that can truly be called seminal. Or could have been, of course, until it came out.

# FOREWORD/AFTERWORD

By Michel Tardieu
*Professor of Structuralist Narratology
at the University of Paris*

Translated by David Lodge

It is a great honour to be invited to contribute a Foreword/
Afterword to this monograph on my distinguished compatriot
and erstwhile colleague, Henri Mensonge. I say 'colleague'
because Mensonge taught for some years at the University of
Paris, though at a different campus from myself – he at Paris
XIV, whereas I teach at Paris I. I do not recall that we ever
actually met, though we must frequently have been present at the
same event – a seminar of Jacques Lacan's, perhaps, or Michel
Foucault's Inaugural Lecture at the Collège de France, or one of
Samuel Beckett's increasingly brief first nights.

As M. Bradbury makes abundantly clear, Mensonge was a shy
and retiring man, who was easily overlooked in a crowd. As his
reputation has grown, so, predictably, has the number of people
who claim to have met him, but these claims invariably turn out,
under scrutiny, to be spurious. There is another group, mainly
members of the Faculty at Paris XIV, who, chagrined at their
failure to recognize his genius when he was among them,
pretend that they never considered his acquaintance worth
cultivating, and some have even gone so far as to deny that he
ever taught at their institution.

For my part, I readily confess that it is a matter of great regret
to me that I never shook the hand of Henri Mensonge, and that
my intellectual relationship with him never ripened into personal

friendship. The reason is simple: by the time I became acquainted with his work, Mensonge had already withdrawn from the Parisian intellectual scene. In fact, it was M. Bradbury's article in the London *Observer* (1 April 1984) that first alerted me to the real importance of that work. Of course one had heard the name mentioned, murmured in the *salons* or passed from table to table in the Left Bank cafés, and *La Fornication comme acte culturel* was one of those books one always meant to read when one had time (time, not so much to read it, as to track it down). But it was not until I came across the seminal article of M. Bradbury's (in a copy of the *Observer* that had been dismembered and screwed up to serve as protective padding for a rare book about the social function of the catamite in classical Greece, which I had ordered from a London bookseller) that the full significance of Mensonge, and his relevance to my own intellectual development, was brought home to me.

Although I occupy a chair of structuralist narratology at the Sorbonne, and am still known to most Anglo-American readers as an exponent of classical structuralism (my method of transposing the plots of classic European novels into quadratic equations is, I understand, a standard component of the curriculum in American graduate programmes and the more academically oriented British primary schools) I have in fact for some years considered myself a *post*-structuralist. The structuralist aim of reducing the chaotic plethora of literary texts to a few elegant and easily memorized tree-diagrams or algebraic formulae now seems to me a utopian dream, an unattainable vision, founded on a false view of rationality and an overestimation of its power to control or subdue the polysemy of language.

Of course, as President Mitterrand was heard to say last New Year's Eve, while waiting for a train (any train) at the strike-ridden Gare du Nord, 'Aujourd'hui, nous sommes tous de nécessité post-structuralistes.' And some of my colleagues have uncharitably suggested that in my recent work I have merely clambered aboard a bandwagon set in motion years earlier by Jacques Derrida and Jacques Lacan. In fact, as I belatedly realized when I smoothed that crumpled page of the *Observer* and began to read M. Bradbury's article, it was Henri Mensonge who

89

had first grasped the fundamental principle of deconstruction, namely, that language ceaselessly undermines its own claim to mean anything, and thus at a single stroke threw the whole structuralist enterprise *en abîme*.

Without knowing it, perhaps, all of us who reached the same conclusion by our own routes had been subtly and indirectly influenced by the example of Mensonge. It was as if, moving almost unnoticed amongst us in the Paris of the early 1960s, Mensonge had left lingering on the air in his wake – haunting as a whistled melody, bewitching as a woman's perfume, potent as grains of pollen – fragments of the discourse of deconstruction which he had already articulated, and which we would later have the illusion of discovering for ourselves. When jealous colleagues accuse me, at some conference or symposium, or in the course of an *Apostrophe* broadcast, of being derivative from Derrida, or of plagiarizing Lacan, I deny the accusation indignantly, but freely admit my indebtedness to Mensonge, a name which invariably throws my opponents into confusion. It is amusing to watch the various expressions of anxiety, fear and low cunning pass across their faces as they ponder whether to admit that they have never heard of him or to pretend that they have and hope that their bluff is not called.

A prophet is not without honour save in his own country. The case of Mensonge bears out the truth of the biblical proverb, and there is a special irony in the fact that the first full-length study of this great French *savant* should have been written by a native of Great Britain, a country, as M. Bradbury himself observes, not noted for its hospitality to new ideas. The ostensible subject of Mensonge's masterwork, *La Fornication*, might have been expected to meet particularly strong resistance from a nation whose capital city has for many years (and long before the advent of AIDS) been plastered with official posters declaring 'No Sex Please, We're British'. In the circumstances, M. Bradbury has done remarkably well. To be sure, his comparative unfamiliarity with French affairs, and French letters, has led him into the occasional minor error or doubtful speculation. It is not true, for instance, as suggested on p.34, that Jacques Derrida revised the

Michelin Guide in 1965. The withdrawal of that year's Guide on account of its unintelligibility was due to operational difficulties with a computerized typesetting system and had nothing to do with deconstruction. Then again, the remark attributed to Mensonge on p.24, 'I ask you never to think of me except perhaps at Christmas,' is almost certainly corrupt, due, I suspect, to some confusion between the French words *Noël* (Christmas) and *nul* (nil, nothing, nobody).

These, however, I must emphasize, are minor blemishes on what is a most valuable and indeed heroic effort to pin down the elusive life and thought of Henri Mensonge. The enterprise is inevitably riddled with paradox and contradiction. How does one describe an author who challenged the very concept of authorship? Drawn inexorably closer and closer to a black hole of epistemological scepticism, the biographer-critic of Mensonge may find his own reality called into doubt. Indeed, the question, 'Who is Malcolm Bradbury?' is hardly less interesting or perplexing than the question, 'Who is (or was) Henri Mensonge?'

The writer who represents himself in Chapter 7 of the present work as a timid and domesticated scholar who eschews the academic jet-set and the international conference scene hardly matches the profile of the Malcolm Bradbury we know from other sources. I have seen with my own eyes the graffito on the walls at the University of East Anglia where he occupies the Chair of American Studies: *What is the difference between God and Malcolm Bradbury? God is everywhere and Malcolm Bradbury is everywhere but here.* There is a suggestive consonance between the syllables 'Bradbury' and 'Bunbury', perhaps the most famous *alias* in the pages of English literature, which persuades me that the name is a floating signifier that has attached itself to many discrete signifieds: Bradbury the campus novelist, Bradbury the Professor of American Studies, Bradbury the Booker Prize judge, Bradbury the TV adapter of postmodernist novelists such as John Fowles and Tom Sharpe, Bradbury the tireless international conference-goer and British Council Lecturer. Even within these separate identities there is doubt and difficulty in establishing the facts – many British readers, for instance, being convinced that the novels of Malcolm

Bradbury are actually written by David Lodge, or *vice versa*.

'Linguistically, the Author is never more than the instance writing.' This profound observation by Roland Barthes, quoted by M. Bradbury, is our best guide in the quest for *his* identity. Subjecting the text of *Structuralism's Hidden Hero* to rigorous stylistic analysis, one cannot fail to recognize two persistently recurring features: the motif of *food* and the rhetorical figure of *bathos*. Furthermore, these two features *invariably occur in the same lexeme*. We find an example in the very first sentence of the book: 'Any bright student or intellectually active person of the 1980s who is at all alert to the major developments in the humanities, philosophy and the social sciences, or is just getting more and more worried why *so many way-out mint-flavoured green vegetables are showing up in a salad these days . . .*' (p.1, *italics mine*). A little later we encounter a reference to 'our chiliasm, our apocalypticism, our post-humanist scepticism, our postmodernism, our metaphysical exhaustion, *our taste for falafel*' (p.5, *italics mine*). On page 42 it is asserted that existentialist cafés in the postwar era resounded 'with cries of *trahison des clercs* and *mauvaise foi*, with or without the *crevettes*', and on page 49, Lacan's re-reading of Freud is described as 'one of the great triumphs of intellectual conversion, comparable to the coming of the McDonald's Hamburger just a few years later'.

It is unnecessary to give further examples – they are to be found on every page. The question is, what does this repeated convergence of food-references and bathos signify? Food is, of course, metonymically associated with digestion and excretion, those functions of the 'lower body' which become instruments of social criticism in Mikhail Bakhtin's theory of carnivalesque (see M. Bakhtin, *Rabelais and His World* [1966]); while bathos is metaphorically associated with the act of falling, or lowering, or dropping. The conclusion is inescapable: *Structuralism's Hidden Hero*, apparently designed to heap praise and honour upon Mensonge and his ideas, is in fact a displaced expression of a deeply repressed desire to cover them with something entirely different. This discovery should occasion no surprise. Most of us who work in the field of contemporary critical theory are subject, periodically, to the same desire.

The post-structuralist project is both inevitable and impossible, and this breeds frustration and aggression in those who are called to carry it out. Inevitable, because once we had eaten the apple, proffered by Saussure, that gave us the knowledge of signified and signifier, there was no recovering that state of primal innocence in which words and things seemed existentially bonded together. Impossible, because (as M. Bradbury elegantly puts it, paraphrasing Mensonge) 'we cannot at once work in language and dismantle it conceptually' (p.63). Jacques Derrida has attempted escape from this *impasse* by the ingenious device of placing words *sous rature* or 'under erasure', signified by crossing them through in the text and thus warning the reader not to accept them at philosophic face value. For instance, in *Of Grammatology* he writes, 'the sign ✗ that ill-named t✗ng, the only one, that escapes the instituting question of philosophy'. The reader of this book would be well advised, before he does anything else, to go carefully through it crossing out every page with diagonal strokes (always provided it is not a library copy).

It is rumoured that Henri Mensonge devised a still more radical method of placing his discourse *sous rature*; that a certain acid was added in the manufacture of the paper on which *La Fornication* was printed which will ensure that sooner or later all copies of this seminal text will auto-destruct. If true, this report would explain why copies of Mensonge's masterwork are so hard to obtain, and render M. Bradbury's account of it uniquely precious.

M.T.

Paris–Birmingham
January 1987

# BIBLIOGRAPHY

Natalie Pelham Barker, 'Mensonge and Feminism', *Broomstick*, VI, Michaelmas 1986, pp. 18–29.

Roland Barthes, 'La Mort de l'auteur', *Manteia*, V, 1968, trans. and repr. in S. Heath (ed.), *Image-Music-Text*, Fontana, 1977, pp. 142–8.

Roland Barthes, *Le Plaisir du texte*, Paris, Seuil, 1970; trans. as *The Pleasure of the Text*, Hill and Wang, 1976.

Roland Barthes, *Roland Barthes par Roland Barthes*, Paris, Seuil, 1975, trans. as Roland Barthes, *Roland Barthes by Roland Barthes*, Hill and Wang, 1977.

Roland Barthes, *Fragments d'un discours amoureux*, Paris, Seuil, 1977, trans. as *A Lover's Discourse: Fragments*, Hill and Wang, 1978.

Georges Bataille, *L'Erotisme*, Paris, Gallimard, 1957.

Jean Baudrillard, *De la Séduction*, Paris, Galilee, 1979.

Jean Baudrillard, *L'Effet Beaubourg*, Paris, Galilee, 1977.

Henry Beamish, 'Mensonge and Charisma', *British Journal of Sociology*, Summer 1972, pp. 35–45.

Harold Bloom, *A Map of Misreading*, Oxford University Press, 1975.

Mstislav Bogdanovich, *Le Cercle de la linéarité*, Paris, Editions de Marge, 1975.

Mstislav Bogdanovich, *Glub*, Paris, Plomb, 1986.

Mstislav Bogdanovich, 'Not So Sure: Current Problems in Semiology', in *The Cunning Linguist*, The Hague, Lambe, 1972.

Mstislav Bogdanovich, 'My(?) Meeting(?) with Mensonge(?)',

*The Times Literary Supplement*, 19 December 1975, p. 1111.

Malcolm Bradbury, 'Terminal Sex', *Observer*, 1 April 1984, p. 23.

Faith Bryers, 'Mensonge and Marie Carrotteuse: A Surmise', *Partisan Review*, LX, 2, Winter–Summer 1981, pp. 5–34.

Michel-Antoine Burnier and Patrick Rambaud, *Le ROLAND-BARTHES sans peine*, Paris, Éditions Balland, 1978.

Anne Callendar, *Mensonge and the Gallo-Scots Literary Imagination*, unpublished Ph.D. thesis, University of Stirling, 1974.

Marie Carrotteuse, 'Mensonge et F. Bryers: une autre surmise', *Flic*, XX, Printemps 1982, pp. 19–34.

Marc Chénetier, ' "J'existe, car je n'existe pas; je n'existe pas, car j'existe": le sens unique double de Henri Mensonge', *Fabula*, 7, pp. 83–92.

Marc Chénetier, 'Les Messages de Mensonge sont-ils les Mésanges du Maussade?: Lyrisme, pessimisme et information chez un précurseur de la déconstruction', *Lu Mule*, XXV, 3, Hiver 1976, pp. 33–52.

Eureca Uri Comturi, 'Le Timbre-poste d'Henri Mensonge', *Fabula Rasa*, XIII, Eté 1983, pp. 48–57.

Maurice Couturier, ' "Unarm, Eros!" ', *Cistre-Essais*, Lausanne, L'Age d'Homme, 1982, pp. 115–23.

Jonathan Culler, *Structuralist Poetics: Structuralism, Linguistics, and the Study of Literature*, Cornell University Press and Routledge, 1975.

Jonathan Culler, *The Pursuit of Signs: Semiotics, Literature, Deconstruction*, Cornell University Press, 1981.

Gilbert Debusscher, 'A la Recherche de l'Imprimerie Kouskous', *EAAS Newsletter*, 5, 1986, p. 3.

Gilles Deleuze and Félix Guattari, *Capitalisme et schizophrénie: L'Anti-Oedipe*, Paris, Minuit, 1972, trans. as *Anti-Oedipus: Capitalism and Schizophrenia*, Viking, 1977.

Jacques Derrida, *Positions*, Paris, Minuit, 1972.

Jacques Derrida, *Signéponge/Signesponge*, (bi-lingual text, English translation by Richard Rand), Columbia University Press, 1984.

Jacques Derrida, *La Carte postale de Socrate à Freud et au-delà*, Paris, Aubier-Flammarion, 1980.

Régis Durand ' "You've Got the Picture?": Negativity and Photography in Mensonge's Early Work', *Shot*, 20–21, Janvier 1981, pp. 124–9.

Umberto Eco, *L'opera aperta*, Milan, Bompiani, 1962.

Umberto Eco, *Il nomma della rosa*, Milan, Fabbri-Bompiani, 1980, trans. as *The Name of the Rose*, Harcourt Brace and Secker, 1983.

Stanley Fish, 'Can We Misread Mensonge?', *Critical Inquiry*, VII, 1, Autumn 1980, pp. 237–49.

Michel Foucault, *Histoire de la sexualité*, Vols. 1– , Paris, Gallimard, 1976ff., trans. as *The History of Sexuality*, Pantheon, 1978ff.

Michel Foucault, 'What Is an Author?' in J.V. Harari (ed.), *Textual Strategies*, cited below, pp. 141–60.

Pierre Gault, 'Mensonge mis à nu', *Trema*, 1, 1976, 33–76.

Josue V. Harari, *Textual Strategies: Perspectives in Post-Structuralist Criticism*, Cornell University Press, 1979, Methuen, 1980.

Millingham Harshly, 'Mensonge and Detective Fiction', *Mean Streets*, March 1974, pp. 12–20.

Ihab Hassan, 'POSTmodernISM', *New Literary History*, III, 1.

Ihab Hassan, 'Mensonge in Milwaukee', *Mensonge Newsletter*, 3, 1978, pp. 2–2½.

Terence Hawkes, *Structuralism and Semiotics*, Methuen, 1977.

Terence Hawkes, 'Troilism and Cressida: Sexeme and Narreme in Shakespeare's Problem Comedies', *Language and Style*, 2, 1973, pp. 40–73.

Terence Hawkes, 'Mensonge in Japan: A Near-Miss', *London Review of Books*, 4 January 1984, pp. 15–19.

Jean-Marie Heurtebise, 'Mensonge Deconstructs', *Post-Nihilist Studies*, IV, Spring 1983, pp. 58–72.

Frank Kermode, 'The Room That Disappeared: An Unfortunate Incident at MLA', *Glyph*, III, Michaelmas 1972, pp. 14–31.

Howard Kirk, 'Mensonge and the Technique of Seduction', *New Society*, 2 October 1972, pp. 8–12.

Julia Kristeva, 'Qui était à Lyon?', *Critique 732*, 1983, pp. 422–48.

Jacques Lacan, 'Lituraterre', *Littérature*, III, 1971, pp. 3–10.

Philippe Lacoue-Labarthe, 'L'Oblitération', *Critique 313*, 1973.

François Laruelle, *Machines textuelles: Déconstruction et libido d'écriture*, Paris, Seuil, 1976.

Vincent B. Leitch, *Deconstructive Criticism: An Advanced Introduction*, Columbia University Press and Hutchinson, 1983.

Claude Lévi-Strauss, *L'Homme nu*, Paris, Plon, 1971.

Claude Lévi-Strauss, 'Le Triangle culinaire', *L'Arc* XXVI, 1965, pp. 19–29.

Andre Le Vot, ' "Kenavo, Déconstruction!"': Mensonge et son ascendance bretonne', *Les Cahiers de St Jean-du-Doigt*, II, 3, Eté 1978, pp. 25–32.

Jean-François Lyotard, *Economie libidinale*, Paris, Minuit, 1974.

Evelyn Maddock, 'Mensonge and "La Petite Grippe" ', *Oxford Magazine*, LXXI, 9, Autumn 1979, pp. 5–7.

Edward Mendelson, 'The Writings of Mstislav Bogdanovich· A Checklist ', *The Times Literary Supplement*, 19 December 1975, p. 1112.

Henri Mensonge, *La Fornication comme acte culturel*, Luxembourg, Kouskous, 1965(?).

Henri Mensonge(?), 'Pas moi', *Quel Tel*, XI, 3, Mai 1968, pp. 11–14.

Felix Messmer, 'The Broken Typewriter of Henri Mensonge', *Cambridge Enquiry*, XIV, Summer 1984, pp. 18–29 [pages 21–2 missing].

T. J. Moran. 'G. I. Vranyovski and Henri Mensonge: Some Unusual Links', *Notes and Hypotheses*, IV, 2, Summer 1984, pp. 12–15.

T. J. Moran, 'Mensonge and von der Luge's *Die Entblössung des Dinges*', *Guesses and Queries*, XI, 8, Summer 1985, pp. 1–3, 89–94.

Jean-Luc Nancy, 'Dum Scribo', *Oxford Literary Review*, 1978, pp. 306–21.

Christopher Norris, *Deconstruction: Theory and Practice*, Methuen, 1982.

Patrick O'Donnell, 'The Pawn Departs: Mensonge on Chess and Intertextuality', *Diuretics*, VI, 6, Spring, 1982, pp. 654–79.

Cleanth Peters, 'Mensonge in Cherry Hinton: A Possibility?', *Granta*, 3, pp. 157–67.

F. Plitplov (Dr), 'A Matter of Whose Umbrella?' *Mensonge Newsletter*, 7, 1972, pp. 7–112.

Claude Richard, 'Mensonge's Unmistakable Stamp', *Delta*, 28, 1986, pp. 111–222.

Edward W. Said, 'Abecedarium Culturae: Structuralism, Absence, Writing', in J. Simon (ed.), *Modern French Criticism*, University of Chicago Press, 1972, pp. 341–92.

Ferdinand de Saussure, *Cours de linguistique générale*, eds. C. Bally, A. Sechehaye and A. Riedlinger, Geneva, 1916, trans. as *Course in General Linguistics*, Peter Owen, 1960.

Ferdinand de Saussure, *Les Anagrammes de Ferdinand de Saussure*, Paris, Paulet, 1968.

Robert Scholes, *Structuralism in Literature: An Introduction*, Yale University Press, 1974.

Bernard Sharratt, 'Rethinking Foreplay from the Beginning', *New Crisis Quarterly*, 1, 1984, pp. ix–xix.

Tom Sharpe, 'Seven Writers I Admire', *Books and Bookpersons*, 344, May 1984, pp. 8–10.

S. N. Sieff, 'A quelle heure arrive-t-il Mensonge à Paris? (When arrive did he Mensonge in Paris?)', *L'Horaire*, VII, pp. 9–12.

Arthur Silent, 'Mensonge Hushed', *Orange-Export*, 2, 1983, pp. 1–3.

Philippe Sollers, 'H.M.', *Quel Tel*, LXVIII, 1971, pp. 19–26.

Laurent Souchu, 'The Gappy Text: An Erotic Reading of *The Bostonians*', *Revue Française d'Etudes Américaines*, IX, 20, Mai 1984, pp. 195–208.

Laurent Souchu, 'En Songe, Mensonge: Oneiric Qualities of Trustworthy Things', *Fabula Rasa*, 6, Juin 1983, pp. 5–25.

John Sturrock (ed.), *Structuralism and Since: From Lévi-Strauss to Derrida*, Oxford University Press, 1979.

René Tadlov, 'The Lie in the Line: Mensonge on Metrics as Hermeneutic Device in Hölderlin, Lindsay and Pound', *Acta Universitas Krakowskaia*, XXXXI, 1975, pp. 51–72; repr. in R. Tadlov, *Gaps, Riffs and Roughs*, Venice, F. Ro di Ziaque, San Marco Verlag, 1977.

Anthony Thwaite, 'Mensonge in Japan: A Palpable Hit', *London*

*Review of Magazines*, Summer 1984, pp. 12–20.

Pierre Vadim, 'La Mort de la fornication', *Cahiers du Cinéma*, XIV, 1969, pp. 10–20.

G.I. Vranyovski [Henri Mensonge?], 'T'ma, mgla, pizda', *Wissenschiften*, XXI, Frühjahr 1982, pp. 17–62.

Evangeline Winthrop, 'Sex in the Head', *Boston Beacon*, 17 May 1975, pp. 4–5.

Michael Woolf, 'Is Mensonge Possible or Not?' *Furtive Review*, XI, Spring 1975, pp. 17–18.

Heide Ziegler, 'Mensonge's Magic Kingdom', *Postfach*, XXI, Fruehaft 1983, pp. 17–28.

Yves Zylot, *Fin*, Paris, PUF, 1975.

# INDEX

Absence, 43–81; compared with presence, 19.

Absurdity, *passim*; Sartre and, 43; Beckett's development of, 47; Robbe-Grillet's rejection of, 49; M.'s putative contact with, 89–91.

Abîme, Mis-en, 27, 39.

Abyss, 37; encounter with, 39.

AIDS, 3.

Althusser, Louis, lack of influence on M. of, 53.

Angoisse, see Angst.

Angst, see Anguish.

Anguish, see Angoisse.

Aporia, 35, 49, 58.

Aristotle, 17, 28; M.'s challenge to, 97.

Author, Death of, 45, 49, 54; inquest on, 57.

Bardot, Brigitte, non-relationship with M. of, 41.

Barthes, Roland, 17, 28–39; teaches M. semiotics, 47; accompanies M. through Alexandrian souk, 59; B. on, 28, 38, 58; B. on B. on, 59; as moralist, 78; as mythologue, 64; as outsider, 78; *Writing Degree Zero*, 78

Beaubourg, 'intestinal architecture' of, 17.

Beaujolais nouveau, compared with nouveau roman, 38.

Beauvoir, Simone de, 39–42; seen with Sartre, 40; seen with M.?, 48; triangular relationships of, 49; feminist implications of, 50.

Beckett, Samuel, 38, 42; war record of, 45; plays with tramps, 47; novels with pings, 49; forced to translate *Finnegans Wake*, 27; feels absurd, 28; absence from own biography of, 48; impact on youthful M. of, 37.

Being, 38; compared with Non-Being, 39; contrasted with Nothingness, 57; questioned entirely, 68; dispensed with totally, 97.

Benjamin, Walter, the 'learned sock' of, 52.

Bloom, Harold, 38; on the rose, 46.

Borges, Jorge Luis, 37; not easy to find, 53–6.

Brasserie Lipp, unsettled bills of M. at, 63.

Breton, André, 32; quarrels with Tzara, 45; makes up, 46.
British Council, influence of Saussure on, 28.
Brooke-Rose, Christine, M.'s hand on knee of?, 56.
Butor, Michel, M's "Manchester" friendship with, 39.

Café Flore, stopped credit of M. at, 64.
Café Rose, M.'s rapid departure from, 65.
Café Royal, M. forbidden entry to, 66.
Camus, Albert, 47, 58; pushes rock up slope, 59.
Cartesianism, see Descartes, René.
Catacresis, see Figures of Speech.
Chabrol, Claude, see Nouvelle Vague.
Clarté, see Lucidity.
Collins, Joan, see Agent.
Cuisine, nouvelle, 27; contrasted with vieille, 34; compared with Mondrian, 27.

Deconstruction, *passim*; end of, 97; replacement by Deleuze, Giles, see Guattari.
De-Deconstruction, 98.
Demystification, see Deconstruction.
Demythologization, see Demystification.
Derrida, Jacques, 37–59, 89–93; productivity of, 38; positions of, 42; slippage in, 45; relation to M. of, 68–77; M.'s deconstruction of, 93; are D. and M. same person?, 114.
Descartes, René, 17, 38.
Desire, Foucault on, 73; Lacan on, 93; M.'s scepticism of, 101.
Diachronic axes, see Synchronic axes.
Differance, Derrida on, 57; Saussure on, 29; what's the, 93.

Ecriture, see writing.
Ecrivain, see writer.
Eliot, T.S., see Pound, Ezra.
Episteme, see Foucault.
Excitement, see Jouissance.
Existentialism, postwar role of, 37; plight and anguish in, 38; café life of, 39; fun really, 40; role of M. Brando in, 41; Structuralist refutations of, 43; M.'s refutation of, 93.

Fornication, la, comme acte culturel, see Mensonge.
Foucault, Michel, on Structuralism, 7; on madness, 37; on power, 47; on absence, 56; episteme of, 68; on self, 69; on sex, 73.
Fourier, Charles, M. says 'not as permissive as he looks', 63.
Freud, Sigmund, on the id, 27; on the ego, 32; on holiday, 53; influence on Structuralism of, 64.

Genet, Jean, unfortunate influence of, 43.
Godard, Jean-Luc, nouvelle vague of, 32.
Grammatology, 38.
*Guardian* newspaper, 7.
Guattari, F, see Deleuze, G.

Hegel, Georg Wilhelm Friedrich, 23.
Heidegger, Martin, 23.
Hemingway, Ernest, 23; drinks bock, 24.
Hermeneutics, *passim*.
Holocaust, 43.

I, is there 1; 38–47.
Identity, 54; questioned, *passim*.
Imprimerie Kouskous, 48–52.

Jakobson, Roman, 27.
John, Elton, 53.
Jouissance, 73, 78; deferred, 83.
Joyce, James, 23; in Zurich, 37; in Paris, 48; in bar, 51; in debt, 52.

Kant, Immanuel, 27.
Kouskous, Imprimerie, see Imprimerie Kouskous.
Kristeva, Julie, asks, was it M., 79.

Lacan, Jacques, mirror stage of, 57; purloined letter of, 73; phallic signifier
    of, 98; M.'s reported comments on doctoral thesis, 'De la psychose
    paranoiaque dans ses rapports avec la personnalité', of, 59.
Laing, R.D., see Parrolle.
Language, *passim*; uselessness of, 17–19.
Langue, see Parole.
Lenin, see Stoppard, Tom.
Lévi-Strauss, Claude, general purpose of, 26; anthropological vision of, 78;
    cooking methods of, 54; rates of exchange in, 58; savage mind of, 67.
Linguistics, *passim*.
Lyotard, J.-F., 23; postmodern condition of, 39.

Macheray, Pierre, 37; over-production of, 83.
McCabe, Colin, not mentioned, 35.
McLuhan, H.M., 46.
Marx, Karl, see Lenin.
Meaninglessness, prevalence of, *passim*.
Metaphor, 27; M. and Derrida, had they?, 63.
Mehlman, Jeffrey, role in indexes of, 81.
Mensonge, Henri, who was he?, 27–38; who says?, 38–43; how do we
    know?, 43–51; what did he do?, 53–71; when did he do it?, 72–4;
    influence of F.R. Leavis on, 75; where is he now?, 93–6; importance of,

*passim*; obscurity of, *passim*; view of fornication, 98–103; seminal role of, 103ff.
Merleau-Ponty, Maurice, after Mehlman in most indexes, 81.
Miller, Hillis, pleasurable response to impact of M., 93.
Mitterrand, François, vol-au-vent of, 16.

Nabokov, Vladimir, strong influence of, 16; major elusiveness of, 72.
Néant, see Being; also Nothingness.
Nietzsche, Friedrich, Derrida on, 89; Foucault on, 90; Elton John on, 23; Hitler on, 97.
Non-Being, compared with Being, 48; differentiated from Nothingness, 49.
Nothingness, contrasted with Non-Being, 49; distinguished from Néant, 52; Sartre's paradoxical view of, 58.
Nouvelle critique, compared with vieille critique, 21.
Nouvelle cuisine, contrasted with food, 23; compared with Mondrian, 27.
Nouveau roman, contrasted with novel, 27; compared with nouvelle vague, 29.
Nouvelle vague, contrasted with cinema, 26; compared with nouvelle cuisine, 28.

Paradigmatic, compared with Syntagmatic, 38.
Parole, see Langue.
Paul, St, 43.
Pensée sauvage, see Lévi-Strauss, Claude.
Perrier, general popularity of, 7, 18, 27.
Phallus, as signifier, 97; as signified, 98.
Picasso, Pablo, paints Gertrude Stein, 48; invents Cubism, 49.
Plaisir, see Pleasure.
Plato, 27; impact on Western thought of, 37, 42.
Pleasure, impossibility of, 48.
Ponge, Francis, only a sign, 89.
Prague School, see Vienna Circle.
Propp, Vladimir, M.'s supposed drinking bout with in Riga, 55.
Pynchon, Thomas, who he?, 89.

*Quel Tel*, M.'s putative appearance in, 75.
Quintilian, *passim*.
Quirk, Randolph, acknowledgements to, xi.

Robbe-Grillet, Alain, new novel of, 33; M. mistaken for, 72.

Salinger, J.D., absence of, 81.
Sameness, see Difference.
Sanity, see Madness.
Sartre, Jean-Paul, 35–8; charismatic role of, 32; philosophical dilemma of, 38; Structuralist reaction to, 41; humanism of, 42; putative friendship of

M. and, 44; has problem with chestnut tree, 49; discovers Non-Being, 50; meets S. de Beauvoir, 52; discovers Being, 53.

Saussure, Ferdinand de, was he really?, 17; on difference, 18; on gaps, 19; posthumous lectures of, 20; student attendance at, 20; his *langue*, 21; his *parole*, 22.

Sémanalyse, Barthes' role in, 38.

Semiotics, 13.

Sens unique, see One Way Street.

Sexuality, 12; end of, 86–97.

Sign, plural meaning of, 38–45.

Signified (*signifié*), absence in Japan, 37; sex as, 58–60; Saussure on, 37; Derrida on, 98.

Signifier (*signifiant*), arbitrariness of, 13; even in Japan, 18; sex as, 58–60; Saussure invents, 37; Derrida changes, 86.

Spielberg, Steven, Deconstructionist film of, 8.

Steak and chips, Barthes' reading of, 46.

Stravinsky, rite of spring of, 42.

Structuralism, *passim*; Saussure invents, 37; Barthes extends, 41; Foucault criticizes, 43; Derrida questions, 49; M. undermines, 45–55.

Stoppard, Tom, travesty of, 32.

Sturrock, John 42; excellent index of, 119.

Sujet, see Subject.

Synchronic, see Diachronic.

Syntagmatic, see Paradigmatic.

Tichbourne, Chidiock, 97.

Traven, B., where is?, 74.

Truffaut, François, see under the new wave.

Tzara, Tristan, finds Dada, 27; discovers Nada, 79.

Unconscious, Freud on, 21; M. found, 84.

Verbal pulsations, 27.

Vienna Circle, see Prague School.

Vol-au-vent, Mitterrand and, 27.

Wilamowitz-Mollendorff, Ulrich von, 99.

Women, circulation of, 23–4.

Wrestling, all-in, 61.

Writing, see Ecriture.

Yale, Gallic influences on, 27; compared with Harvard, 38; M.'s putative chair at?, 49.

Zeno, 112; confesses, 113.

Zeugma, see Figures of speech.